2016

He straightened, looking like a nervous stallion scenting a mare, wanting to grab her and flee from her at the same time.

His eyes had darkened like a stormy night as his warring needs fought inside him. He didn't bolt.

But he made no move toward her, either. Instead, he fisted his hands at his sides. A slight hitch in his breathing was all that she needed to know that she had a chance to win this battle.

She rose to her feet, keeping her eyes locked on his the whole time. Slowly, she padded across the thick carpet to stand in front of him, with only a few inches and the heat from both their bodies between them.

"Colton," she whispered. "I want you."

He swallowed, his Adam's apple bobbing in his throat. "We're working on a case. We don't have time—"

"We do have time. Hours to kill." She slid her hands up the front of his chest, delighting in the feel of his muscles bunching beneath the thin fabric of his T-shirt. "And I've got the perfect way to spend at least one of those hours."

"Silver…" His voice came out a harsh rasp. He cleared his throat and tried again, still not touching her, hands at his sides. "I'm not what you're looking for."

"Now, that's where you're wrong, Colton."

Deep Cover
Detective

LENA DIAZ

First Published in Great Britain 2016
By Mills & Boon, an imprint of HarperCollins*Publishers*
1 London Bridge Street, London, SE1 9GF

Large Print edition 2016

© 2016 Lena Diaz

ISBN: 978-0-263-06663-0

Our policy is to use papers that are natural, renewable
and recyclable products and made from wood grown
in sustainable forests. The logging and manufacturing
processes conform to the legal environmental
regulations of the country of origin.

Printed and bound in Great Britain
by CPI Antony Rowe, Chippenham, Wiltshire

Lena Diaz was born in Kentucky and has also lived in California, Louisiana and Florida, where she now resides with her husband and two children. Before becoming a romantic suspense author, she was a computer programmer. A former Romance Writers of America Golden Heart® Award finalist, she has won a prestigious Daphne du Maurier Award for Excellence in mystery and suspense. To get the latest news about Lena, please visit her website, lenadiaz.com.

This story is dedicated to
Sean and Jennifer Diaz. My greatest,
most rewarding accomplishment in life
is having amazing children like you.
I'm so proud of you both.

Thank you, Amy, Diana, Gwen, Krista,
Manda, Rachel, Sarah and Sharon.
KaTs rule.

Thank you, Angi Morgan and
Alison DeLaine, for daily laughs
and the magic room.

And, as always, a sincere thank-you
to my editor and agent, Allison Lyons
and Nalini Akolekar,
for their constant support.

Chapter One

Colton shook his head in disgust and thumped the nav screen on his Mustang's dashboard. It had to be broken. Either that or the GPS tracker he'd tucked under Eddie Rafferty's bumper in Naples was on the fritz. Because if the screen was to be believed, the budding young criminal had driven his car off the highway and directly into south Florida's million-and-a-half-acre swamp known as the Everglades.

Driving a car into the saw grass marsh and twisted islands of mangrove and cypress trees was impossible unless the car was sitting on pontoons. And Eddie's rusted-out vintage

Cadillac boasted bald tires just aching for a blowout. Not a pontoon in sight.

Colton pulled to the shoulder of I-75 near mile marker eighty-four, just past a low bridge over a culvert. This was the last location where the navigation unit showed Eddie's car before it had taken the turn toward the swamp. So much for using technology to follow the suspect. He should have stayed closer, keeping Eddie in sight instead of relying on the GPS tracker. But when the kid had taken the ramp onto the interstate, Colton had worried that Eddie might get spooked seeing the same black Mustang in his rearview mirror the whole time he was on the highway. So Colton had dropped back a few miles.

Where was the juvenile delinquent now? Certainly not on the highway, and not on the shoulder. Heck, even if the GPS was right and he *had* pulled off the road here, there was nowhere else to go. Eight-foot-high chain-link fencing bordered this east-west section of I-75 known as Alligator Alley. The fence kept the wildlife from running out onto the road and causing accidents. And yet the dot on the dashboard screen still showed Colton's prey continuing south, *past* the fence.

He eyed the tight, solid-looking chain-link mesh twenty feet away. No holes, no skid marks on the asphalt to indicate that a vehicle had lost control. The safety cable along the bottom was intact. But he supposed that could be misleading.

Twice now, that he knew of, vehicles had managed to go airborne after clipping a guardrail and had sailed over the cables and slid under the chain links—without triggering the cable alarms that would automatically notify the police and the department of transportation to send help. Had the same thing happened to his burglary suspect? If it had, the GPS would show him as stationary. And yet that dot just kept moving. Had a gator swallowed the tracker on

Eddie's bumper and was swimming down one of the canals?

Determined to figure out exactly what was going on, Colton got out of the car and stepped to the edge of the road. And that was when he saw it. *Another* road. Single lane and parallel to the highway, it was set at a slightly lower elevation than I-75, making it nearly impossible to see when driving past unless someone was specifically looking for it. The road turned a sharp right before the fence, heading back in the direction that Colton had just come from. It went down an incline, toward the culvert beneath the bridge where wildlife could cross to the other side of the highway without interfering with traffic.

The culvert, of course.

That must be where Eddie had gone. Maybe Colton hadn't been as subtle as he thought he'd been when following the kid back in town and Eddie realized he had a tail. So he'd hidden out down there, waiting for Colton to pass him by.

An even better scenario would be that Eddie *didn't* know he was being followed, and he'd just accidentally led Colton to his secret hiding place for his stash of stolen goods. This could be the break Colton had been looking for. If he caught Eddie red-handed, he would have the leverage to coerce him into revealing the identity of the burglary ring's leader. The case could be wrapped up in a matter of days. And then Colton could go back to his normal life for a while, at least until the next big assignment came along and he had to go undercover again.

Excitement coursed through his veins as he ran back to his car. He hopped inside and yanked his pistol out of his ankle holster, automatically checking the loading before placing it in the console. He didn't think Eddie had crossed the line yet to becoming a gun-toting criminal, but he wasn't betting his life on it. Be Prepared might be the Boy Scouts' motto, but it was Colton's, as well. He had no desire to end up on the wrong side of a nervous, pimply-faced teenager's gun without firepower of his own at the ready.

He wheeled the car around and followed the mysterious road that he must have passed a hundred times over the years and never known was there. But after reaching the bottom of the hill, instead of continuing, the road turned a sharp left and dead-ended at the chain-link barrier with a line of tall bushes directly behind it. And the culvert on the other side was clearly empty. No sign of Eddie or his car.

Colton's earlier excitement plummeted as he pulled to where the road stopped so he could turn around. But before he could back up, a section of the fence started rolling to the right, along with the bushes, which he now realized had been cleverly attached to what was actually a gate. The bushes must be fake, since they weren't planted in the ground. And they were obviously someone's attempt to obscure the view, so others wouldn't realize what Colton could now clearly see—that the road did indeed continue south into the Glades.

It was narrow, and mostly gravel, but it was dry and elevated a few feet above the marsh that bordered it on both sides. It curved into the saw grass, probably by design to help hide it. But a section of it was just visible about fifty yards away, where it headed into the pine and live oak that began a thick, woodsy part of the Glades.

Figuring the gate might close on him while he pondered his next move, he pulled forward to block the opening. Then he called his friend and supervisor in the Collier County Sheriff's Office, Lieutenant Drew Shlafer. After bringing Drew up-to-date on the investigation and the discovery of the hidden road, Colton was disappointed in Drew's lack of surprise.

"You know this road?" Colton asked. "You know where it leads?"

"You said it's just past mile marker eighty-four, right? Opposite a culvert?"

"Yeah. So?"

"Ever heard of Mystic Glades?"

"Rings a vague bell. Isn't that where some billionaire crashed his plane a few months ago?"

"Dex Lassiter. He ended up smack-dab in the middle of a murder investigation, too. But that's a story for another day. Mystic Glades is the small town at the end of the road that you found, the same town where Lassiter ended up, a few miles south of the highway. The residents are a bit…eccentric…but mostly harmless. From what I hear."

"Mostly? From what you hear? You've never been there?" Colton accelerated through the gate. Just as he'd expected, it slid closed behind him as he drove down the winding road.

"Never needed to. It's rare for the police to get a call from a Mystic Glades resident. They tend to take care of whatever problems they have on their own. There have been a few hiccups recently, like with Lassiter. But other than that, the place is usually quiet."

"There's no permanent police presence?"

Colton glanced at the nav screen as he headed around another curve. The screen blinked off and on. He frowned and tapped it again.

"The people of Mystic Glades don't really cotton to outsiders, or police. Although I hear they're starting to cater a bit to tourists that have heard about the place because of Lassiter's case. Still, I wouldn't expect them to exactly welcome anyone unless they bring the almighty dollar with them and plan to leave without it. But don't worry. You're in an unmarked car and you've gone grunge, so I doubt they'll even look twice at you. They might even think you're one of them."

Colton rolled his eyes and glanced at his reflection in the rearview mirror. Grunge wasn't his thing, but the description wasn't too far off for how he looked right now. Since going undercover, he'd let his dark hair grow almost to his shoulders and worked diligently every morning to achieve a haven't-shaved-in-days look without letting it get out of control and become an itchy beard. His usual military-short hair and clean-shaven jaw would be a red flag to the types of thugs he'd been hanging with lately. They'd smell "cop" the second he walked through the door, thus the unkempt look. His new look did have the advantage of making getting dressed every morning a no-brainer. A pair of jeans and a T-shirt and he was good to go. Not like his usual fare of business suits that he wore as a detective.

"Just how far off the interstate is this place? I've gone about three miles and all I see are trees and saw grass." A black shadow leaped from the ditch on the right side of the road just a few feet in front of his car. He swore and slammed his brakes, sliding to a stop. But whatever he'd seen had already crossed to the other side and disappeared behind some bushes.

"You okay?" Drew asked.

"Yeah. Something ran out in front of me. I'd swear it was a black panther, but that doesn't seem likely. They're pretty rare around here."

"Nothing would surprise me in Mystic Glades. But I'd be more worried about the boa constrictors people let loose out there once they get too big and eat the family dog. And gators, of course. Watch your step when you get out of the car."

Colton could hear the laughter in Drew's voice. He could just imagine the ribbing he'd get at their next poker game if he *did* manage to tangle with a snake or gator. Assuming that he lived to tell about it.

"You sure you don't want to trade places?" Colton asked. "You sound as if you're having way too much fun at my expense."

Drew didn't bother hiding his laughter this time. When he quit chuckling, he said, "You couldn't get me out there if you held a gun to my head. There's a reason I traded undercover work long ago for an office. I like my snake-free, air-conditioned, pest-free zone. Did I mention how big the palmetto bugs are in the Glades? It's like they're on steroids or something."

"Don't remind me. That's why my last girl-friend left me. She couldn't handle the humidity or the giant bugs here in Florida."

"Serves you right for dating a Yankee. And for picking up a woman while on vacation at Disney World. What did you expect? Wedding bells?"

Colton grinned and started forward again, keeping his speed low so he wouldn't accidentally veer off the narrow path into the water-clogged canals now bordering each side. He didn't mind Drew teasing him about Camilla. Dating her had been a wild whirlwind of fun. Exactly what each of them had wanted. Neither of them had expected it to last. He had no intention of ever leaving Florida and offered no apologies for his modest, blue-collar roots. And Camilla's perfectly manicured toes were firmly planted in the upper-crust society back in Boston.

It had been a hot, sweet, exceptionally plea-surable three weeks and they'd parted friends, but with no plans to reconnect in the future. With the kind of life he led, that was for the best. Disappearing for months at a time while undercover didn't create a foundation for an enduring relationship. And he loved his job far too much to consider giving it up, at least not for a few more years.

"Another thing to look out for," Drew said. "I've heard that electronics go kind of wacky around there."

Colton thumped his GPS screen, which alternated between showing a moving dot and blacking out every other second. "Yeah, I see that."

"Cell phones are especially unreliable out there. Except maybe in a few choice spots. You might not be able to get a call out for backup if something goes wrong. Keep that in mind before jumping into anything. When you check back in with me, you'll probably have to head outside Mystic Glades to do it."

"Understood." He drove around another curve and then pulled to a stop. Directly in front of him on an archway over the road was an alligator-shaped sign announcing the entrance to Mystic Glades.

He inched forward, then stopped again just beneath the archway, blinking at what seemed like a mirage. "You're not going to believe this," he said into the phone. "Mystic Glades looks like someone took an 1800s spaghetti Western town and plopped it right into the middle of the Everglades. I'm at the end of a long dirt-and-gravel road with a line of wooden buildings on either side. Instead of sidewalks, they've got honest-to-goodness boardwalks out front. Like in horse-and-buggy days."

The phone remained silent. Colton pulled it away and looked at the screen. No bars. No signal. The call had been dropped. Great. He put the phone away and checked the GPS. That screen was dark now, too. Useless, just as Drew had warned.

He debated his next move. Going in blind didn't appeal to him, with no way to let his boss know if he needed help. But working undercover often put him in situations where he couldn't call for days or even weeks at a time. So this wasn't exactly new territory. Plus, the kid he was after was just a few days past his eighteenth birthday and still had the lanky, gangly body of a teenager. Physically, he wasn't a threat to Colton's six-foot-three frame, and probably had half his muscle mass, if that. But if Colton discovered the other members in the burglary ring out here—and their leader—he could be at a huge disadvantage by sheer numbers alone, not to mention whatever firepower the group had.

His undercover persona so far hadn't managed to get him inside the ring, but he'd been living on the streets in Naples where most of the burglaries had occurred, developing contacts. And he'd heard enough through those contacts, along with his team's detective work back at the station, to put the burglary ring at around fifteen strong, possibly more. He even knew the identities of a handful of them. But without being sure who their leader was, and having evidence to use against him, Colton needed some kind of key to break the case open. Right now that key appeared to be the group's weakest link, Eddie Rafferty. A small fish in the big pond, Eddie would be the perfect bait to draw the others out. But to use him as bait, first Colton had to catch him.

Even though he didn't see the rust-bucket Caddy anywhere, he might have caught the break he needed. Because little Eddie Rafferty had just stepped out of a business called Callahan's Watering Hole and was sauntering toward the far end of the street.

Time to go fishing.

Chapter Two

Silver stood in the front yard, shading her eyes from the sun as she faced the whitewashed two-story—her pride and joy, the first bed-and-breakfast ever to grace Mystic Glades. Thanks to the recent success of Buddy Johnson's airboat venture that was bringing in tourists and the dollars that went with them, all but one of her eight bedrooms was booked for the next three months, starting tomorrow, opening day.

Bright and early, Tippy Davis and her boyfriend, Bobby Jenks, would be here to help Silver after Buddy's airboats brought the B and B's first guests. Everything was ready—except for attaching the large sign to the part of the roof that jutted out over the covered front porch with its gleaming white railings.

"A tad to the left, Danny," she called out to one of the two men on ladders beside the front steps, holding either end of the creamy yellow, bed-shaped sign that announced Sweet Dreams Bed & Breakfast, proprietor Silver Westbrook.

"Looks perfect where it is, if you ask me."

She smiled at skinny Eddie Rafferty, who'd just walked up. The beat-up junker that he was so proud of was nowhere to be seen. Since he lived several miles away, deep in the Glades, she figured maybe he'd parked his car in the lot behind the building next door, Mystic Glades's answer to Walmart, Bubba's Take or Trade.

"You think it's centered?" she asked.

"Yep."

"Stop right there," she called out. "Eddie said the sign's perfect."

Danny gave them both a thumbs-up, and the sound of hammers soon shattered the early-morning quiet. Snowy egrets flushed from a nearby copse of trees and the razor-sharp palmetto bushes that separated her little piece of town from Bubba's and the rest of the Main Street businesses. On the other side of her B and B, more trees and lush, perpetually wet undergrowth formed a thick barrier between the inn and Last Chance Church. Beyond that, there was only the new airboat dock and the swamp with its ribbons of lily-pad-clogged canals.

She loved the illusion of privacy and serenity that the greenery provided, along with the natural beauty that her artist's soul craved. Being this close to nature, instead of seeing concrete and steel skyscrapers out her attic-bedroom window every day, was one of the reasons she'd returned to her hometown after being gone for so many years. *But not the only reason.*

"You're right, Eddie. It's perfect. You have a good eye."

He flushed a light red and awkwardly cleared his throat. It practically broke Silver's heart knowing how much her compliments meant to Eddie. He was like a stray cat. Once offered a meal or, in her case, friendship and encouragement, he'd made a regular habit of making excuses to visit her.

Unlike a stray, he wasn't homeless. But since he'd turned eighteen a few weeks ago and was technically an adult, he *would* be homeless soon. His foster parents, Tony and Elisa Jones, were anxious for him to move out so they could put another foster kid in his bedroom and continue to receive their monthly stipend from the state. Eddie was supposed to be looking for a job every day in Naples, but Silver suspected he was up to something else entirely. Probably hanging out with the wrong crowd, like Ron Dukes or Charlie Tate, the two little hoodlums she blamed for half the trouble that Eddie got into.

In spite of their friendship, Silver didn't know all that much about him except that, unlike her, he hadn't grown up here. She knew he didn't have any blood relatives. But whenever she'd tried to get him to open up about his past, he would shut down and disappear for days. So she'd stopped asking.

Town gossip, assuming it could be trusted, said that Eddie had spent over half his life in the foster system. And for some reason, even though there had been interest off and on, no one had ever adopted him.

It was a chicken-and-egg kind of thing. Did he continually get into trouble because he didn't have a family, or did he not have a family because he kept getting into trouble? Either way, he was too young to be thrown away like a piece of garbage. He had potential, and she fervently hoped he would turn his life around one day, before it was too late.

Danny Thompson and his friend exchanged a wave with her as they folded their ladders and headed back to Callahan's. Buddy was probably champing at the bit for Danny's return. The morning airboat tours couldn't start without him to pilot one of the three boats. But Danny had insisted there was plenty of time to help her hang the sign before the boats were due to push off. After all, the tourists were enjoying the "free" breakfast portion of the tour package right now at Callahan's.

It was a point of contention between Fredericka "Freddie" Callahan and Labron Williams, the owner of Gators and Taters, the only official restaurant in town. Callahan's was a bar, and had added the "grill" part of their service only after Buddy decided to add breakfast as a stop on his daily tours. Labron felt the tours should have breakfast at his place and was furious with Freddie for undercutting his bid. But, secretly, Silver believed that Labron—who'd always run a lunch-and-dinner-only place anyway—just wanted an excuse to see Freddie every day, thus the melodramatic feud going on between them.

"I brought something else that I think will look good in your inn," Eddie said.

She noted the brown bag tucked under his left

arm and had to fight to hold on to her smile. *Please don't let that be another expensive piece of art that I know you can't afford.*

He pulled a short, thick, cobalt-blue vase out of the bag.

Oh, Eddie. What have you done now?

Unable to resist the urge to touch the beautiful piece, she reverently took it and held it up to watch the sunlight sparkle through it. The color was exquisite, so deep and pure it almost hurt to look at it. She'd never seen anything like it and was quite sure she never would again. It was a one-of-a-kind creation. And probably worth more than she'd earn in a month. She carefully lowered it and handed it back to him.

"It's gorgeous. Where do you manage to find such incredible pieces?"

"Here and there," he answered with a vague wave of his free hand while he hefted the vase in the other, making her heart clutch in her chest at the thought of him dropping it. "Do you want it or not?"

Yes. *Desperately.* She absolutely adored all things blue. Opening her eyes every morning to the sun filtering through that thick glass and reflecting the color on the walls of her bedroom would be like waking up in heaven. But she could never afford it. Still, letting it go wasn't an option, either. No telling where the vase might end up, and whether its new owner would realize how precious it was or be careful to keep it from harm.

Once again, she'd have to become the temporary caretaker of a priceless piece of art to keep it from falling into someone else's hands, at least until she could figure out how to return it to its rightful owner—along with several other pieces Eddie had brought to her over the past few months. If he ever suspected what she knew about him, and her ulterior motives for coming back to Mystic Glades, he'd disappear faster than a sandbar in high tide. And then she'd have no way to protect him or help him out of the mess he was making of his life.

"How much?" she asked, careful not to let her disappointment in him show in her voice.

He chewed his bottom lip, clearly debating how much he thought he could get. "Fifty dollars?"

She blinked in genuine surprise. He had no clue what that vase was worth. Add a couple more zeroes to the end of his fifty-dollar price and it would be much closer to the true value.

"Forty-five?" he countered, probably thinking she was shocked because the price he'd asked was too *high*.

Knowing that he'd expect her to bargain with him, she shook her head and played the game. "I can't afford that, not with all the expenses of opening the inn. I just spent a small fortune at the Take or Trade to get a shipment of fresh fruit and vegetables for my guests tomorrow." She eyed the blue vase in his hand again. "Will you take…thirty?"

The rumble of an engine had them both looking up the street to see a black muscle car of some kind heading toward them. Silver didn't recognize it, so she assumed it was probably a tourist. But even that seemed odd, since most tourists didn't drive here—they came by airboat, courtesy of Buddy's new tour company. Almost no one but the residents of Mystic Glades could even find the access road off Alligator Alley.

"Thirty's fine." Eddie's gaze darted between Silver and the approaching car. He tended to be shy and nervous, even around people he knew. So she could understand his trepidation around a stranger. But was there something more to it this time? He seemed more nervous than usual.

"You can pay me later. I'll put the vase inside." He jogged to the steps and rushed into the B and B, letting one of the stained-glass double doors slam closed behind him.

Silver winced, half-expecting the glass inset to shatter. When it didn't, she let out a breath of relief. It had taken her weeks to design and painstakingly put together the glass in those doors. And she didn't have the money to fix anything until her first paying customers arrived tomorrow.

Or until payment for her *other* job was deposited into her banking account.

She turned around as the black car pulled into one of the new parking spots she'd had paved just last week—with real asphalt instead of the dirt and gravel that dominated the rest of the town. Just one more thing to set her inn apart, a diamond in a sea of charcoal. Not that she minded charcoal. She'd made many a sketch with paper and charcoal pencil, some of which were hanging on the walls inside. But she wanted her place to sparkle, to be different, special. She'd paid, and was still paying, a hefty price for the inn. She needed everything to be perfect.

As she watched the sporty car, the driver's door popped open and a cool-drink-of-water of a man stepped out. Silver's concerns about Eddie faded as she appraised the driver, studying every line, every angle, appreciating every nuance the same way she would any fine piece of art. Because he was definitely a work of art.

Graphite. If she sketched him, that was what she'd use—a graphite pencil across a dazzlingly white sheet of paper. The waves in his shoulder-length, midnight-black hair would look amazing against a bright background. And that stubble that stretched up his deeply tanned jaw? She could capture that with a pointillism technique, then shade it ever so carefully to emphasize his strong bone structure.

Her fingers itched with the desire to slide over his sculpted biceps not covered by his ebony, chest-hugging T-shirt. The curves of those muscles were perfect, gorgeous, the way God meant them to be. And his lips...they were sensual, yet strong, and far too serious. She would want to draw them smiling. Otherwise, the black-and-white sketch would be too severe, intimidating. Yes, definitely smiling.

She tapped her chin and studied the narrowing of his waist where his dark T-shirt hung over his jeans. Did he have one of those sexy V's where the abdominal muscles tapered past his hips? She'd bet he did. And his thick, muscular thighs filled out his faded jeans as if they'd been tailored—which maybe they had. A man like him, so tall and perfectly proportioned, probably couldn't buy off-the-rack.

Scuffed brown boots peeked out from the ragged hem of his pants, making her smile. A cowboy in the Glades. That might be a fun way to draw him, maybe with a lasso thrown around that big stuffed gator Buddy had recently put in his store, Swamp Buggy Outfitters, to draw in tourists. She'd have to add a hat, of course. Or she could change those boots to snakeskin and draw him—

"Ma'am? Hello?"

She blinked and focused on his face. He must have been talking to her for a moment, but she hadn't heard him. No surprise there. Happened all the time. He stood a few feet away, his thumbs hooked in his jeans pockets, watching her with a curious expression.

As she fully met his gaze for the first time, something inside her shifted beneath an avalanche of shock and pleasure. His eyes…they were the exact shade of cobalt blue as the vase. They were, quite simply, amazing. Beautiful. Incredibly intriguing. Her fingers twitched against her palms as if she were already grasping a pencil. Or maybe a paintbrush.

His eyes widened, and she realized she still hadn't said anything. "Sorry, hello," she said. "I tend to stare at people or things and zone out."

The almost-grin that curved his sensual lips seemed to be a mix of amusement and confusion—an unfortunate combination of emotions that she was quite used to people feeling around her. When she was a child, it had hurt her feelings. As an adult, she felt like telling people to just grow up and deal with it. So she was different. So what? Everyone was different in one way or another. That was what made the world interesting.

He motioned toward the inn. "Yours?"

"Yep. You looking for a place to stay?"

"What makes you think I'm not a local?"

She laughed. "Not only are you not a local, you've never been here before or you'd know that was a silly question. There are only a few hundred residents in Mystic Glades. And there's not a stranger in the bunch. We all know each other."

"What about that young man I saw go inside a minute ago? You know him, too?"

Her smile faded. Was this one of the men Eddie was mixed up with? This man, as ruggedly gorgeous as he was—looked like the wrong crowd, dangerous even. She crossed her arms. "Why do you ask?"

He shrugged. "Just testing your theory—that you know everyone. Maybe he's a tourist like me. Doesn't matter." He held out his hand. "I'm

Colton Graham. And if you've got a room available tonight, I'd appreciate a place to stay."

She reluctantly shook his hand, not quite ready to trust his claim of being a tourist. "Silver Westbrook."

Still, if he *was* a tourist, then his interest in Eddie was probably just harmless curiosity, nothing she really needed to worry about. And that meant that she didn't have to feel guilty for wanting to enjoy the play of light across the interesting planes of his face. She rarely painted anymore, preferring to sketch with pencil or charcoal, sometimes pen, without all the mess or work involved with setting up her paints and then cleaning up afterward. But the best way to capture him might be with paint, perhaps watercolors.

"Ma'am?"

She blinked. "Sorry. Spaced out again, didn't I?"

The almost-grin was back. "Yeah, you did. Is something wrong? You seem preoccupied."

"No, no. Everything's fine." She waved her hand impatiently, tired of having to explain her unfortunate quirks to everyone she met.

At his uncertain look she sighed. "I get lost in shapes, textures, colors. I can't help it."

"Ah. You're an artist. I know the type. My sister does that a lot." He smiled, a full-out grin this time that reached his incredible blue eyes. And completely transformed him, just as she'd thought it would. Smiling, he looked approachable, warm, *perfect*. She *had* to put him on canvas. It would be a sin not to. And she wouldn't use watercolors. They were too muted for this vibrant man. No, acrylics…that was what she'd use to capture every detail in vivid color.

Her gaze dropped to his narrow waist. "Have you ever modeled?" she asked. "I'd love to paint you nude. I would pay a sitting fee, of course. I'm a bit strapped for cash right now, but I could let you stay a night without charge and call it even."

He made a strangled sound in his throat and

coughed. "Um, no, thanks. That's not really my thing." He waved toward the inn again. "But I *would* like to rent a room for the night, if you have a vacancy."

Swallowing her disappointment, she glanced around, suddenly very much aware of how alone the two of them were and how separated the inn was from the other businesses. The street was deserted, with most of the residents out of town at their day jobs or inside the local businesses. The idea of taking this man, this complete stranger, into her home had her feeling unsettled.

"You don't have any vacancies, then," he said, interpreting her silence as a no.

"It's not that. Actually, the grand opening is tomorrow. I hadn't really planned on renting out any rooms tonight."

He waited, quietly watching her.

Why was she hesitating? This wariness was silly. If she was going to run a bed-and-breakfast, she'd have to get used to renting rooms to people she didn't know. And drop-ins were bound to happen. It certainly wouldn't be nice to turn him away when she was fully capable of offering him a place for the night. And the extra income was always welcome.

"Okay, why not?" she said. "But don't expect me to cook for you today. That starts tomorrow, when my help arrives."

"I'm sure I'll figure something out so I don't starve."

His smile was infectious, and she couldn't help smiling, too. "Just one night, then?"

He glanced toward the front doors, then in the direction of the airboat dock about fifty yards away, which was barely visible from here. Or maybe he was looking at the church with its old-fashioned steeple and bell that the ushers rang by pulling on a rope every Sunday morning at precisely nine o'clock.

"Just tonight," he said.

His rich baritone sent a shiver of pleasure up her spine. He really was an exquisite specimen of male. And she really, *really* wanted to paint him. Maybe she could ask him again later to model for her and he might change his mind. And if she could convince him to stay longer than one night, she'd have more chances to try to sway him into modeling for her. Plus, starting tomorrow, the place would be full of other people. Any concerns about being alone with a man she didn't know wouldn't matter at that point. When it came down to it, more important than the painting was the *money*. A fully rented inn was far better than a partially rented one.

"If you want to stay just one night, that's okay," she said. "But there are only eight rooms and seven are booked solid for the season. I expect the last one will get snatched up pretty fast once the first group of guests begins to spread the word about their stay here. If you don't take it now, it might not be available later in the week."

"You're quite the saleswoman. Okay, I'll book

a week. Might as well. Never been in the Everglades before and this looks like a great spot."

Yes! That put her at 100 percent occupancy. She couldn't ask for a better start to the business she'd been saving her whole life to start. And her other job would be over soon, God willing, so that income wasn't something she could rely on indefinitely. Every penny counted now.

"Aren't you even going to ask the price?" She crunched down the gravel path toward the front doors with him keeping pace beside her.

"That was going to be my next question."

She gave him the particulars and he handed her a credit card before holding one of the doors open for her.

"Sounds more than reasonable," he said.

"Great. And thanks," she said as she stepped through the door he was holding. She led him to the check-in desk beside the staircase. She took an impression of his credit card on an old-fashioned carbon paper machine and set it on the counter for him to sign.

"Haven't seen one of those since I was a little kid," he said as he took the pen from her and scrawled his signature across the bottom.

"Yeah, well. You do what you have to do without reliable internet and phone service. Don't worry, though. There are hundreds of movies in the bookshelves in the great room for you to choose from if you want to watch something while you're here. I've got the classics along with tons of newer titles in all genres. And each guest room has its own TV and DVD player."

"Sounds good." He pocketed his credit card and scanned the lobby as if he was looking for someone. Then he suddenly grew very still, his gaze settling on something behind her.

Fearing that a wild animal had somehow managed to sneak inside, Silver whirled around. No furry attacker was waiting to jump at her. But what Colton was staring at was just as dangerous...*for Eddie*.

The network of cubbies on the homemade bookshelf that spanned the wall behind the desk held the blue vase prominently in the middle where Eddie must have placed it. And that was where Colton's gaze was currently riveted. A shiver shot up Silver's spine at the intensity of that look. And this time it wasn't a good shiver.

Without asking her permission, he rounded the desk and hefted the vase in his right hand. "This is…beautiful. Where did you get it?"

Beautiful? She'd bet her last sketch pad that he'd been about to say something else and stopped himself. Did he recognize that piece? Suspect that it was stolen?

After taking the priceless vase from him, she set it back in the cubby. "I bought it from a friend. I'd appreciate it if you wouldn't pick up any pieces of art that you see around here. Some of them have been in my family for generations."

"But not that one." He eyed it as if he was itching to grab it again.

"You seem quite interested in that." She waved

toward the cubby. "Do you have one like it back home, wherever home is?"

"Atlanta, Georgia. And no, I don't. But I'd like to. This…friend you bought it from. Do you think I could meet him? Maybe see if he has another one for sale?"

"What makes you think my friend isn't a woman?"

He shrugged. "Him. Her. Doesn't matter. My sister recently bought a new house and I've been meaning to pick her up a housewarming gift. I know she'd love something like that." He pointed to the vase. "She adores bright colors. Like I said earlier, she's an artist, too."

Sure she was. Silver doubted the man even had a sister, or that he lived in Atlanta. His story sounded too pat, as if he'd quickly made it up to cover his unusual interest in the vase and his sudden appearance in Mystic Glades—just a few minutes after Eddie had approached her. Coincidence? Maybe. Maybe not.

"How did you happen to find the entrance to

our little town?" she asked as she recorded his name in the registration book. "It's unusual for anyone but residents to know that exit."

He shrugged. "Honestly, it was an accident. I ran over some debris on the highway and pulled to the shoulder to check my tires. That's when I saw the exit. Figured I might as well take it and see where it led. After all, I'm on vacation. Have all the time in the world."

His story was plausible, she supposed. But the timing of his arrival, along with his interest in the vase, still bothered her. Did he have a hidden agenda for being here? He seemed like a man with a purpose, not the kind who'd randomly pull off a highway and take a gravel road that seemed to lead nowhere. She sorely regretted having rented him a room for the night, let alone the whole week.

"About that vase—"

"Sorry. Can't help you." She snapped the registration book closed and grabbed a key from the drawer underneath the counter. "The person

I bought it from isn't around right now. Here's your key, Mr. Graham." She plopped it in his hand. "Your room is upstairs, room number eight, last one on the right."

Unfortunately, his room was right beneath *her* room in the converted attic, with the door to the attic stairs right next to his door. That was far too close for comfort. But all the rooms were decorated with specific themes, and the guests chose the themes they wanted when they made their reservations. She couldn't reassign them.

Maybe she should drop into Bubba's Take or Trade and buy a lock for her bedroom door. If Colton ended up snooping while he was here, he might discover the other items that Eddie had brought her, including several in the attic. Until she could be certain *why* he was so curious, and whether he was a threat, she'd have to be very careful.

"As I mentioned earlier, there aren't any formal meals planned for today," she continued. "But you're welcome to make full use of the kitchen." She waved toward the swinging door to the left of the entry. "I'm sure that you'll find everything there you could possibly need. You certainly won't starve. And there are toiletries in the bathroom attached to your room—shampoo, soap, even a toothbrush and toothpaste in case you didn't think to bring them. Do you have any luggage you'd like me to get for you?"

His eyebrows rose. "I'll get my bag myself in a few minutes. Thanks. I'll just go up and check out the room first." He headed toward the stairs to the right of the desk.

Silver hesitated as he disappeared down the upstairs hallway. She worried about the attic and whether he'd snoop. But she had a more important errand to do right now than babysit her first guest.

She hurried to the front door, determined to find Eddie.

And warn him.

Chapter Three

Colton leaned back against the wall upstairs, just past the open banister, waiting. Sure enough, the inn's front door quietly opened below, then clicked closed, just as he'd expected. He jogged to the stairs and caught a glimpse of Silver Westbrook through one of the front windows as he headed down to the first floor. Her shoulder-length bob of reddish-brown hair swished back and forth, a testament to how fast she was going as she turned right.

She looked like a little warrior, ready to do battle as she marched up the street—except that he couldn't quite picture her holding a weapon while wearing a tie-dyed purple-and-lime-green poncho with bright blue fringe brushing against her tight jeans. And the flash of her orange tennis shoes would be like a beacon to the enemy on a battlefield, just as it was a beacon to him.

The woman certainly wasn't subtle about her love of color. The fact that the outside of the B and B was white was the real surprise, because the inside was just as colorful as Silver's outfit—a mix of purple, blue and yellow hues on every wall, and even on the furniture. But instead of being garish as he'd expect of an inn decorated with that palette, somehow everything combined to work together to make the place feel warm, inviting. She really did remind him of his artistic sister. Too bad the two would never meet.

Because Silver Westbrook would probably end up in prison when this was all over.

Once she was a few buildings up the street, he headed out the door after her. But instead of skirting around the backs of buildings to follow his prey, he forced himself to walk up the street in plain sight. He didn't want anyone looking out a window to think he was anything but an interested tourist exploring the town. And all the while he fervently hoped that Silver wouldn't turn around and realize he was following her.

The concern in her eyes, and the wariness when he'd foolishly grabbed that vase, had put him on alert that she knew far more about its origins than she was letting on. And he'd figured she would want to go warn whoever had sold it to her as soon as he was out of the way. That was why he'd gone upstairs. And sure enough, she'd bolted like a rabbit.

He regretted that he'd shown his interest in the piece. He'd just been so stunned to see it that he hadn't managed to hide his surprise. That blue vase was at the top of his stolen goods sheet and worth several thousand dollars. The owners were anxious to get it back. And Colton was anxious to catch whoever had stolen it.

The fact that the vase had been taken two

nights ago in Naples and ended up here today, along with Eddie, couldn't be a coincidence. He really, really wanted to get that little hoodlum in an interrogation room and get him to roll over on his thug friends. But now there was another wrinkle in the investigation.

Whether Silver Westbrook was part of the burglary ring.

He would hate to think that a woman as intriguing and beautiful, and smart enough to run her own business, would get involved in illegal activities. But how else could he explain how defensive she'd gotten when he'd asked about Eddie and, later, the vase, unless she knew she'd accepted stolen property?

From the moment he'd met her and had been the recipient of such a brazen evaluation of his…assets…and then propositioned to pose nude so she could draw him, she'd fascinated him. Her tendency to space out and get lost in her own little artist's world was as adorable as it was frustrating. He'd love to get to know her better, find out what other unique quirks she was hiding, and how her fascinating artist's mind worked—which wasn't going to happen if he ended up arresting her.

And that was what made this whole trip so frustrating. Because he was pretty sure that if things turned out the way it looked as though they would, he'd end this day by hauling both Eddie and Silver to jail.

Near the end of the street, almost all the way to the archway that marked the beginning of Mystic Glades, she turned right, jogged up the steps to the wooden boardwalk and went inside one of the businesses. The same business where Eddie had been earlier, Callahan's Watering Hole. Coincidence? Not a chance. Silver was definitely going there to find the kid, probably to warn him that a stranger seemed far too interested in his whereabouts and the stolen goods he'd brought with him.

Colton increased his stride and hurried to the same building, which appeared to be a bar, based on the name and the tangy smell of whis-key that seemed to permeate the wooden siding. He couldn't worry about stealth now. He had to hurry to catch both of his suspects before they managed to disappear completely.

His boots rang hollowly across the wooden boardwalk. He pushed the swinging doors open, bracing himself for something like a line of sa-loon dancing girls and drunken patrons lined up at the bar, even though it was still morning. After what his boss had told him about Mystic Glades, and what little he'd seen for himself, nothing could surprise him.

He stopped just past the opening. Okay, wrong. He *was* surprised, surprised that every-thing seemed so *normal*.

The mouthwatering, sweet smell of sugar-cured bacon hit him as his eyes adjusted to the dark interior and more details came into focus. There weren't any saloon girls or patrons at the bar guzzling whiskey. But the place *was* packed, and from the looks of the cheap, souvenir-shop types of Florida T-shirts on most of the people sitting at little round tables throughout the room, they were mostly tourists. This must be why the street out front was so deserted. Everyone was in here, eating breakfast.

There was no sign of Silver, though.

"Are you part of the airboat tour group?" a well-endowed young woman in a tight T-shirt and short shorts asked as she stopped in front of him, a tray of drinks balanced on her shoulder and right hand.

"No. I'm alone."

"Okay, well, there are a couple empty seats over there." She waved toward a pair of vacant tables near the bar. "I'll take your order as soon as I give these airboat peeps their refills."

"Thanks."

"Thank me with your pocketbook, sugar." She winked and bounced off to a table on the far side of the room, her long blond ponytail swishing along with her hips.

Good grief. She didn't look old enough to

serve alcohol, let alone dress like that or flirt with him. He looked away, feeling like a perv for even noticing the sway of her hips. Hopefully she was older than she seemed. But one thing was for sure—*he* felt far older than his thirty-one years right now.

He scanned the tables again, more slowly this time, the booths along the right wall, the short hallway on the left side of the room, just past the bar. But there was no sign of Silver. And no sign of Eddie, either. He eyed the set of stairs directly in front of him that ran up the far wall. A red velvet rope hung across the bottom with a sign on it—Employees Only. Was that where she'd gone? If not, she had to be in the kitchen, or in one of the rooms down the hallway.

Maybe he was too late and she'd already ducked out a back door. He decided to check the hallway first, to see if that was where the door was. But all he found were the restrooms, which he presumed had no exits. He did a quick circuit of the men's room and then paused outside the ladies' room, debating whether he should check it, as well.

"Something wrong with the men's room?"

He turned, surprised and also relieved to see Silver standing about ten feet away, at the opening to the hallway. *She hadn't gotten away.* Her eyes, which he'd already realized were a fascinating shade of gray, a *silvery* gray—her namesake perhaps?—narrowed suspiciously and her hands were on her hips. Or maybe Silver was a nickname because of her taste in jewelry. Right now she had on silver hoop earrings and a long silver necklace.

A peacock. Her unique, colorful ensemble—topped off with purple laces on her left shoe and neon green laces on her right—reminded him of a beautiful peacock with its feathers spread in all their glory. That made him want to smile, which only made him irritated. *She's a suspect, Colton. Get a grip.*

"Just checking the place out," he said, seeing no benefit in giving up his cover just yet, not without knowing where Eddie was and whether she'd warned him. "I was curious what was down this way."

"Right. Was there a problem with your room at the inn? Is that why you followed me?"

The accusation in her tone, in every line of her body, swept away his earlier amusement. *She* was the one accepting stolen property *at best*; in league with the robbery ring at worst. And she was acting as if *he* was in the wrong? He was tempted to take his handcuffs out of his back pocket and put an end to this charade right now. But there was too much on the line to let his anger, justifiable or not, rule his actions. He needed to play it cool, try to calm her fears and, if possible, make her trust him.

He stopped directly in front of her. "Okay, you caught me. I didn't actually go into my room. I changed my mind and thought I'd explore the area first. And when I noticed you going in here, I figured—" he smiled sheepishly "—I *hoped*, maybe I could catch you and convince you to have breakfast with me." He braced an arm on the wall beside her and grinned. "After all, you did ask me to take off my clothes. Sharing a meal is nothing compared to that."

Her eyes widened and her face flushed. Good. He'd knocked her off balance. And hopefully deflected her suspicions. If he could get her to believe he was interested in her, then maybe she'd think his earlier questions had been an excuse just to talk to her.

It wasn't as if he really had to pretend. He *was* interested in her. If he wasn't on the job right now, and didn't believe she was mixed up in criminal activity, there'd be no question about his intentions—he'd pursue her like a randy high school teenager after his first crush. Because Silver Westbrook was exactly the kind of woman he liked—beautiful and smart. And unlike his last fling, Camilla, Silver was a Florida native. And she was blue-collar, like him. On the surface, there didn't seem to be any reason to keep them apart.

Except for a little thing called grand theft.

"That *is* why you came in here, right?" he said. "To eat?"

Now *she* was the one looking as though she was worried that he'd caught her in a lie.

"Of course," she said. "Yes, I'm here for breakfast. Starving. Let's find a table."

She practically ran to one of the empty tables near the bar, and Colton followed at a more sedate pace, trying not to let it bother him that she seemed so anxious to get away from him. Man, he really needed to focus here—on the case, not on the way she made his blood heat as he sat across from her.

They quickly ordered. Just a few minutes later, a brawny man in his mid- to late-thirties helped the overworked waitress by bringing Colton and Silver's food to their table. Faded tattoos decorated his massive arms, intricate patterns of loops and swirls that meant nothing to Colton. But the ink did—it looked homemade, like the kind convicts used in prison.

Colton nodded his thanks while he studied the man's face, automatically comparing it to the wanted posters back at the station. The cook nodded in acknowledgment, his dark eyes hooded and unreadable as he returned to the kitchen through a doorway behind the bar without saying a word.

"Who is that guy?" Colton asked.

Silver shrugged. "Can't say I've ever talked to him. I think his name's Cato. He's one of the new guys from out of town that Freddie hired to help out with our little tourist boom."

"Freddie?"

"Fredericka Callahan. She owns the place." She waved toward one of the larger tables on the opposite side of the room. "She's the elderly redhead arguing with the elderly bald guy."

"Arguing with a customer doesn't seem good for business."

"Labron Williams isn't a customer. He owns Gators and Taters on the other side of the street, a little farther down toward the B and B. I'm pretty sure he came in here just to gripe with Freddie."

"Gators and Taters?"

"Uh-huh. They like each other."

"The gators?"

She rolled her eyes. "Freddie and Labron."

He glanced toward the rather odd-looking pair. Freddie was built like a linebacker. Labron would probably blow away in a stiff wind and was a foot shorter than her. And while Freddie's unnaturally bright shock of red hair was rather loud, it had to compete with Labron's bald pate that reflected like a headlight beneath the bright fluorescents overhead, as if he'd just applied a thick coat of wax and polished it until it shone.

"But they look like they want to kill each other," Colton said.

"That's because they like each other."

She casually took a sip of water as if nothing about their conversation seemed strange. Then again, maybe to her it didn't.

"Why did you ask about Cato?" She set her

water glass down and pinned him with her silvery gaze.

Colton was still trying to figure out why two mature adults who "liked" each other would face off like a pair of pit bulls over a bone. But Silver's question about the cook had him focusing on what was important—not blowing his cover as a tourist.

"No reason. I was just curious. He doesn't seem to fit in with everyone else around here." He waved toward the waitress. "Neither does she. Too young. Did Freddie hire her from out of town, too?"

"No. That's J.J., Jennifer junior. She's lived here all her life. She's J.S.'s daughter, on summer break from college. She graduates next semester from the University of Florida. A year late, unfortunately, but at least she hung in there."

The young waitress was old enough to have already graduated from UF? *Thank God*. Now he didn't feel *quite* as bad for noticing her figure. "J.S. Jennifer...senior?"

"No, silly. Jennifer *Sooner*. She used to live closer to town but just built a cabin about five miles southwest of here, not too far from Croc Landing."

Croc Landing. Why would someone name a place Croc Landing around here when there were only a few hundred crocodiles in south Florida and probably a million alligators? He decided not to ask. No telling where that conversation might lead.

He took a bite of eggs, and was pleasantly surprised at how fluffy and delicious they were. Maybe ex-con Cato had learned some cooking skills while he was in prison.

As the two of them ate, the silence between them grew more and more uncomfortable. For his part, he kept thinking about the case and was annoyed that the intriguing, sexy woman across from him chose to be a criminal. For her part, he supposed, she was trying to figure out why he was here and who he really was.

By the time J.J. arrived with the bill, they were both so desperate to end the stalemate that they grabbed for the check at the same time.

Colton plucked it out of Silver's hand. "I've got this."

"Thank you," she snapped.

"You're welcome," he bit out.

J.J.'s eyes got big and round as she glanced from one of them to the other. As soon as Colton handed her his credit card, she scurried off like a puppy afraid it was about to be kicked.

An older man who'd been making the rounds from table to table, talking to each group of tourists, stopped beside Silver and gave her a warm smile. "Who's your new friend, young lady?"

Colton didn't figure he needed an introduction. It was pretty hard to miss the man's name, since it was written in big white letters across his dark brown T-shirt.

"Hey, Buddy," Silver said. "He's a guest at the inn. Colton Graham, meet Buddy Johnson, owner of Swamp Buggy Outfitters next door, the airboat operation down the street, and a handful of other businesses. He practically runs the town."

He puffed up with self-importance, reminding Colton of that peacock he'd likened Silver to earlier, but minus all the colorful plumage. This man had arrogance stamped all over him. But he must have some redeeming qualities, too, because Silver appeared to like him.

"I wouldn't say that," he corrected Silver as he shook Colton's hand. "But I'm definitely vested in our little piece of the Glades." He put his hand on the back of Silver's chair. "I thought the inn didn't open until tomorrow."

"It doesn't. Not officially. But Mr. Graham needed a place to stay so…" She shrugged.

Buddy eyed him speculatively. "Decided to come see the Everglades, have you? First time in Florida?"

"No. I've come here every summer since I was a kid." And fall and spring and winter, too.

"Ever been on an airboat tour, Mr. Graham?"

"Can't say that I have." Another lie. Normally, hiding the truth wasn't a big deal. It was part of his job. But for some reason, lying to this white-haired man was making him uncomfortable. It was like lying to his grandfather.

"Well, then. I insist that you take a tour." He waved toward the other tables. "I run airboat tours daily. Picked this passel up this morning at the main dock twenty miles south of here. We're heading out in a few minutes. Three boats, plenty of room. Come along. I'll give you ten percent off for being a guest at the inn. Silver and I offer cross-promo discounts, since I bring guests to her inn, starting tomorrow, that is. But I'll give you a discount a day early."

"That sounds like a *great* idea." Silver sounded way too enthusiastic as she smiled at Colton. "The airboats are the best way to see the Everglades. You should go."

The reason behind her eagerness to get rid of him was pathetically obvious. While he was gone, she'd probably rush to have a powwow with her criminal friends. His fingers itched to grab her shoulders to shake some sense into her and ask her why she was so foolishly throwing her life away.

"I'll think about it." He had no intention of going on a tour. He planned to keep Silver in his sights.

"Now, son. There's no time for thinking. The tour is going to take off in a few minutes. And you won't want to miss out. You're going." Buddy nodded as if it was a done deal. "And, Silver, since he's your guest, you can both sit together on the same boat."

Her eyes widened. "Ah, no. I'm not going to—"

"I've been trying to get you on one of my tours for weeks," he interrupted. "This might be your only chance this season, since the inn opens tomorrow and you'll be busy after that. You'll come, right?"

"I really don't think that I can…"

His face fell with disappointment.

Silver's shoulders slumped in defeat. "Okay. I'll take the tour today. But I'm sure that Colton has other plans."

"I wouldn't miss it for the world."

Her narrowed eyes told Colton exactly what she thought of his sudden change of heart.

"Excellent," Buddy said, grinning with triumph. "You can both pay the cashier at the dock. Make sure you tell her about the discount." He waved his hand in the air and headed toward another table.

Silver frowned after him.

"He basically forced you into taking a tour," Colton said. "And he's still going to charge you for it."

"Yeah. I noticed." Her voice sounded grumpy. "I'll have to return the favor if he ever wants to stay at the inn."

Colton grinned. And, surprisingly, Silver smiled back. For a moment, they were simply a man and a woman enjoying each other's company, sharing their amusement at Buddy Johnson's tunnel-vision focus on making a buck, even at a friend's expense—quite literally. But then Buddy's voice boomed through the room, telling the tour group it was time to go. Silver's smile faded and she looked away. The magic of the moment was lost.

"Let's go, let's go, ladies and gents," Buddy called out. "We need to get going before the skeeters and no-see-ums start biting."

Chairs scraped across the wooden floor and the buzz of voices echoed through the room. The tourists headed toward the front door like a herd of elephants, waved on by three men dressed in khaki shorts and brown T-shirts the same color as Buddy's, but instead of their names across the front, there were logos of airboats with the company name, Buddy's Boats.

The last of the tourists headed out. Silver

mumbled something and hurried after them. She and Buddy were out the swinging doors before Colton could stop her. He had to wait for the waitress, who was heading his way with his credit card and one of those ridiculous carbon papers for him to sign. This place really was stuck in a different decade.

After taking care of the bill and thanking J.J., he hurried outside. The tourists were already halfway down the street. Buddy had Silver by the arm and was talking animatedly about something while she nodded.

Good, she hadn't managed to escape.

Chapter Four

In spite of Buddy's promise to ensure that Silver and Colton could sit together on one of the three boats, Silver did her best to thwart that plan. Since the boat that Danny Thompson was captaining was the most full, she hopped on it and almost squealed with triumph when she got a seat without any empty ones close by. But, at the last minute, the man beside her got up and hurried to a different boat. And who should plop down in his place but Colton Graham.

As he settled beside her, his broad shoulders rubbing against hers, she glanced toward the man who'd just left and saw him shoving one of his hands into his pocket. The flash of green paper left no question as to what had just happened.

"You bribed that man to let you sit here," she accused.

His very blue eyes widened innocently. "Why would I do something like that?"

Since she couldn't answer that without voicing her suspicions about the vase and Eddie, she didn't bother to reply. Instead, she looked out over the glades as the boat pushed away from the dock, and she did her best to ignore her unwanted neighbor.

Once out in the middle of the waterway, the giant fan on the back of the boat kicked on. Any questions Colton might have planned on asking her would be difficult at best to ask now. She gave him a smug smile before turning away.

When they reached an intersection of canals, the boats split up, each going down a different waterway. Buddy grinned and waved at her from one of the other boats and she returned his wave, unable to fault or even resent him for pressuring her into this trip.

He'd been asking her all summer to take one of the tours so she could recommend them when her B and B guests asked about the airboat rides. Today really was the last realistic chance this season for her to take the tour. And without him bringing a boat of B and B guests every morning as agreed, the chance of her inn flourishing, or even surviving, was practically zero. She owed Buddy a debt of gratitude that he'd come up with the idea once she mentioned her desire to start the B and B.

She glanced at Colton, who was studying the passengers rather than the twisted, knobby-kneed cypress trees they were passing. Everything about him seemed…off. He wasn't acting like a tourist. A feeling of alarm spread through her every time he looked at another one of the handful of men and women on their boat, as if he was memorizing their faces or looking for something. Or someone.

Who *was* he? An insurance investigator trying to save his company money by finding that vase? A family friend of the vase's rightful owner? Or, worse, one of Eddie's so-called friends who was looking to settle some kind of debt? Her fingers curled around the edge of the seat cushion beneath her as her mind swirled with even worse possibilities, including the very worst—that he might be a cop.

That would ruin everything.

He turned and caught her staring at him. And just then, Danny cut the engine, dramatically dropping the decibel level as the loud fan sputtered and slowed and then fell silent. Great. Just great.

"We'll drift here for a few minutes so you can catch some gator action or maybe see some cranes fishing for an early lunch," Danny announced. "We'll tour the salt marsh after that."

A low buzz of excited conversation started up around them as the others took out their cameras and phones and began pointing and clicking.

"About that vase—" Colton began.

"Don't you want to take some pictures?" she interrupted. "There's a gator sunning himself on the bank over there. You'll probably never get another chance to take a picture this close without getting your arm bitten off."

"Seen one gator, you've seen them all."

"I thought you've never been to the Everglades before."

"There's this thing called a zoo," he said drily.

"Don't you live in Georgia?"

"I do."

"Atlanta, right? Like your sister?"

He frowned at her. "I'm pretty sure that I already told you that. Why?"

"I've been to Zoo Atlanta. They don't have gators."

He gave her a smug smile. "Then you haven't been there lately. They brought in four from Saint Augustine this past year."

She had no clue whether he'd made that up or not. But she had a feeling he was telling the truth. Which meant…what? That he really was from Atlanta?

"About the vase—"

"Where in Atlanta? I have friends there. Which subdivision?"

He let out an impatient breath. "No subdivision, just some land outside town."

"Where?"

One of his eyelids drooped. "Where what?"

"Where's your land?"

He cleared his throat. "Peachtree. Can we get back to my question about—"

"Peachtree." She laughed. "Seriously? Everything in Atlanta is on Peachtree. Which Peachtree?"

He stared at her, his dark, brooding eyes and serious expression making no secret that he was frustrated with her evasion of his questions. Finally, he let out a deep breath and opened his mouth to say something else.

Silver quickly turned to the woman sitting on the other side of her and tapped her shoulder. "Look." She pointed toward the bank. "There's a snowy egret. Ever seen one of those before?"

The woman's eyes widened and she grabbed her camera. "It's so pretty!"

As the woman snapped pictures, Silver told her everything she knew about egrets, which turned out to be a lot, since she'd grown up in the area. On her other side, she heard another one of Colton's deep sighs, and when she carefully turned ever so slightly a few minutes later to see what he was doing, he was staring out at the bank on his side of the boat. Good, maybe he'd finally give up trying to ask her questions. She could keep up her conversation with the other woman and maybe even some of the other tourists if she had to in order to survive the boat ride. But what was she going to do once they got back to the inn?

She'd figure *something* out.

Maybe she should invent some kind of disaster—like a burst pipe in a wall—to get him to leave. No, that would cause real harm to the inn and she couldn't afford that. The air conditioner? She could take a fuse out or something to get it to quit cooling. That would make the place miserably hot as the sun got higher in the sky this afternoon. Yes, maybe that would work.

Danny used a long paddle to edge them closer to the bank on Colton's side and pointed out several different species of plants to his picture-snapping audience.

"What the…" Suddenly Colton raised his left arm in front of her and angled his body so that his back was to her.

"Stop the boat against the bank," someone yelled. The voice sounded as though it came from the shore. And it sounded…familiar.

Someone in the boat screamed.

Silver leaned over to see what was happening.

On the bank about ten feet away, beneath a twisted cypress tree, a man stood with a bandanna tied across his face with holes cut out for the eyes. On his head was a Miami Marlins baseball cap. And in his hand, pointed directly at Danny, was a gun.

Excited chattering erupted all around as the tourists began to realize what was going on. Danny did as he was told, poking his guide pole beneath the water into the mud to push the boat toward the bank. A low grinding noise sounded as the bottom of the hull scraped across weeds and mud, then stuck and held.

The gunman rushed over to the boat but didn't try to board. He aimed his pistol at Danny and pitched a large burlap bag into the boat. "Jewelry and cash," he said. "Fill it up. Hurry."

Oh, no. She suddenly recognized the voice. *Eddie, what are you doing?* She groaned and shook her head.

Colton moved his left hand down between them, the back of his fingers skimming her calf as he slid the leg of his jeans up his boot.

Silver blinked with horror when she saw

why. He had a gun. It was strapped in a holster against the side of his boot.

She grabbed his arm just as his fingers closed around the gun. "What are you doing?" she whispered.

He jerked his head around and frowned at her. "I'm a cop," he whispered. "I'm an undercover detective with the Collier County Sheriff's Office. Don't worry. It's okay."

A cop? Her stomach sank. Everything had just gotten a whole lot more complicated. And dangerous. *He was about to ruin everything.* She had to stop him. She shook her head back and forth. "Too dangerous," she whispered back. "Someone could get hurt."

"Someone could get hurt or *killed* by that kid holding the pistol. Now stay down." He pushed her hand off his arm.

Silver clenched her fists. Danny was passing around the burlap bag while Colton slowly pulled his gun out of the holster, his gaze never leaving Eddie.

This was a disaster waiting to happen. She *had* to protect Eddie. The gun in Eddie's hand was shaking so hard Silver was afraid he was going to shoot someone by accident. And Colton had his gun completely out of the holster now.

Silver leaned back and raised her right hand as if swatting away a bug. The movement caught Eddie's attention, as intended. His head swiveled her way, and his eyes widened. Silver made a gun signal with her pointer finger and thumb and pointed at Colton's back. It didn't seem possible, but the gun in Eddie's hand started to shake even more. He nodded, and Colton snapped his head around to look at her suspiciously.

She dropped her hand from behind his back and gave him a nervous smile.

His eyebrows slashed down and he whipped his head back toward Eddie.

"Your jewelry, Silver," Danny said, pushing the bag toward her.

She hesitated, glancing from Colton to Eddie.

They were staring at each other like two gun-men about to have a shoot-out.

Do something. You have to stop this before someone gets hurt.

Silver started to pull her necklace over her head.

Eddie turned his gun away from Danny and toward Colton.

Colton started to bring his gun up.

Silver dropped her necklace and it clattered against the floor of the boat in front of Colton. "Oh, darn it. Sorry." She braced her right hand on his shoulder and leaned across him.

"Out of the way," he snapped.

"Sorry, sorry, oops." She fell across his lap, slamming her right arm on top of his gun arm and trapping it between her breasts and his lap.

She jerked her head up and looked at Eddie. *Go,* she silently mouthed to him.

He whipped around and ran for the trees.

Colton swore and tried to yank his gun out from beneath her, but she clung to him like pine sap on a brand-new paint job. He looked toward the bank, then shook his head and looked back at her. His glare was so fierce she was surprised she didn't turn into a human torch on the spot.

"I should arrest you right now," he growled. "You let him get away on purpose."

"I fell." She blinked innocently and braced her hands on his thighs, pushing herself upright.

He swore viciously and let his gun slide back into the holster, then yanked his pants leg down over it. No one seemed to have even noticed his gun. The rest of the passengers were all chattering excitedly. And Danny had turned away to try to comfort a loudly crying woman.

Colton leaned down toward Silver, his face a menacing mask of anger. "Until I figure out my next step, you keep quiet. Not a word to anyone about me being a cop or I *will* arrest you. Got that?"

Bristling at his tone but understanding his anger, she decided to comply—for now—and gave him a curt nod.

He crossed his arms and looked away, as if he couldn't stand the sight of her anymore.

A hand touched her left shoulder. The woman who'd been so excited by the egrets earlier looked ready to pass out. Her eyes were like round moons brimming with tears about to spill down her cheeks.

Her lips trembled as she whispered, "I can't believe we were almost robbed. We could have been killed."

Silver's heart tugged at the poor woman's fear. Her own anger at Eddie probably rivaled Colton's anger with her. Thank God, no one had gotten shot, but that didn't mean they hadn't been hurt. This poor woman, and others, would probably have nightmares and no telling what other lasting effects because of Eddie's stupid stunt. Silver squeezed the woman's hand and pulled her into a hug, rocking her and patting her back as she tried to soothe her.

"You'll want to take the boat to the main dock where everyone's cars are parked." Colton's deep voice cut through the conversations around them as he addressed Danny. "We'll have cell phone coverage there and can call the police to report the gunman."

Danny hesitated, then nodded. "Right. Of course. Um, ladies and gentlemen, my apologies for the fright you just had. The tour is over. We're returning to the south dock." He gave Colton another curious look before using the pole to push the boat off the mud.

Chapter Five

Colton switched his cell phone to his other ear and leaned against the police cruiser as he and his boss debated his next move. The airboat captain had brought the tourists to this main dock near the Interstate. This was where the tourists had parked their cars earlier this morning before being taken in the boats to Mystic Glades for breakfast.

Half a parking lot away, on the mini-boardwalk outside Buddy's Boats Boutique, a team of four Collier County Sheriff's deputies were interviewing the few remaining airboat riders. Most of them had already given their statements and had been allowed to go. Only Silver, Danny Thompson and a couple of others were left.

A different group of deputies had taken one of the department's airboats out earlier, with Danny as their guide, to the spot where the gunman had been, in order to search for clues. But other than some muddy footprints that the soggy marsh had rendered useless as evidence, there wasn't much to find. And no trace of the gunman. They'd brought Danny back and now those deputies were already on their way back to Naples.

As Colton listened to Drew, some of the store's staff members came outside on another one of their rounds, checking on everyone and passing out bottles of water—at four bucks a pop. Colton supposed that was entrepreneur Buddy Johnson's brand of Southern hospitality.

"Okay," Drew said. "Since the B and B owner interfered and it's unlikely the perp even saw your gun, what do you think had him spooked?"

"Miss Westbrook must have signaled him,

warned him, just before she threw herself on me so I couldn't draw my gun."

"You think she interfered on purpose?"

"Yes. But I can't prove it. When I drove into Mystic Glades and saw Eddie talking to her, I should have confronted her then and there. Instead, before I continued to the B and B, I waited to see what they would do. Eddie disappeared. And Miss Westbrook's been playing cat and mouse with me ever since. Did she interfere on purpose? I'd bet my next raise on it."

"All right. Then how do you want to play this?" Drew asked.

He'd already given it some thought and knew exactly what he wanted to do. Namely, get out of Mystic Glades. "Once all the passengers have been interviewed, the airboat captain is going to take Miss Westbrook and me back to the dock in Mystic Glades. Once there, I'll arrest her and drive her to the station for an interrogation. And while I'm working on getting her confession, one of our guys can get a search warrant for the inn. My statement that I saw that blue vase should be good enough to get a judge's signature."

He kept an eye on Silver while his boss considered his recommendation. She seemed to have made it her personal mission to help the mostly older crowd of tourists after each one of them was interviewed by the police. She hugged them as if they were old friends, put her arms around their shoulders and helped them to their cars. Anyone watching her would think she was a saint and that she really cared about those people. And yet she was covering for the man who'd pointed a gun at them. It didn't make sense.

"What about Rafferty?" Drew asked. "Can you peg him as the gunman?"

Colton thought about it. "My gut tells me it was him. But he had his entire face covered, and since he wore a ball cap, I couldn't even tell you his hair color. No way could I swear in court that it was him. A defense attorney would hear me describe the guy as Caucasian, aver-age height and build, and then he'd remind the jury that half the people in the country could be described that way."

"All right. Then, basically, this is where I think we stand. Your cover as a tourist is still intact with everyone except Miss Westbrook. If we can ensure her silence, you can still hang around Mystic Glades and try to get in with the town gossips, or maybe listen in at the bar you mentioned. Someone is bound to know where Rafferty's hiding and give him up. Then you can confront him, lie, tell him we've got his prints at one of the burglarized homes or some-thing. Get him to roll over on the ringleader."

Colton straightened away from the police car. "Hold it. What are you saying? There's no way we can trust Westbrook."

"Maybe, maybe not. You told her not to tell the other tourists that you were a cop. From what you've said, she's kept her word."

"Only because either I or one of the other

deputies has been with her the whole time. She hasn't had an opportunity to spill the truth. We have no way of knowing whether she'll continue to keep quiet."

"Then you'll have to stay with her. Don't let her out of your sight."

"Drew—"

"It's not a request, Colton. You've spent months and plenty of resources on this case. Other than pegging a few minor players that we agreed wouldn't have access to the man at the top of the food chain, we've got nothing. We were putting all our chips on Rafferty because he seemed knee-deep in this thing and might lead us to the higher-ups. But if he was the gunman today, then it's a safe bet that he's going to lie low for a while. I want you to try to flush him out, but we have to consider that the ship may have sailed. Which leaves us with Westbrook as our only link to the whole ring. That's the angle you need to work."

"I can *work* it by hauling her to the station and interrogating her."

"Or you can go back to the bed-and-breakfast, threaten to arrest her for interfering with a police investigation if she doesn't cooperate, then step back and see what happens. If she thinks the jig is up, she'll want to warn the other members of the burglary ring. My guess is she'll do that after she thinks you're asleep. So follow her. See where she goes."

Colton shook his head in frustration. Drew's plan was too risky. Rafferty had already gotten away and might not be seen again. What if Silver slipped away, too? It would be far safer to take her into custody right now. And although he'd never admit it out loud to Drew, in spite of everything that had happened, he was worried about her.

He knew her type, how her creative mind worked, from growing up with a sister much like her. To Silver, the world was a fascinating, enchanting place full of interesting people and things to study and capture in some kind of medium. She judged people based on their faces, voices, maybe even the colors they wore. She put faith and trust where it wasn't always warranted. To someone like her, "bad guys" could be hard-luck cases and she felt sorry for them. He doubted she saw true evil in anyone. And that made her particularly vulnerable.

In spite of how angry she'd made him by risking her life and throwing herself on him when he was pulling out his gun, he was also shaken that he could have hurt her. And damn it, he didn't want her hurt. Even though she frustrated the heck out of him, and was likely involved with the criminals he was after, she didn't strike him as a "bad" person. His instincts, honed from years of working with some of the worst excuses for humanity out there, told him that by most people's measures she was probably a "good" person who'd gotten caught up in something and didn't know how to get out of it.

But that didn't mean he'd go easy on her. She

needed a wake-up call before she got hurt or her misplaced loyalties got someone else hurt.

"Colton? You still there?" Drew asked.

"Unfortunately. I still think that bringing her in is the better plan, the safer one."

"When you're the boss, you can make that decision. Until then, give our B and B owner enough rope to hang herself. Let her lead you to the burglary ring leader and end this thing once and for all."

SILVER SPENT THE airboat ride back to Mystic Glades trying to think of some way to get rid of Colton Graham. Since throwing him overboard would likely get her arrested or force her to jump into the gator-infested swamp to save him, she discarded that notion, no matter how tempting. And she couldn't think of a reasonable excuse to toss him out of the B and B, nothing that wouldn't raise his suspicions even more than they already were.

She'd expected him to barrage her with questions the whole trip back, but instead he'd stared out over the water and occasional spans of saw grass and trees, as if he were deep in thought. Even the scores of alligators they passed, lying on the banks sunning themselves, didn't shake him from his silence.

A few minutes later, Danny cut the noisy engine and steered the boat toward the landing. As soon as it bumped against the dock, Silver was out of her seat. But before she could hop out and leave her unwanted guest behind, his right hand clamped around her left wrist like an iron band.

She shook her arm, trying to make him let go. "What are you doing?"

"We need to talk." He stepped onto the dock and helped her out, but then his hand was around her wrist again, an unbreakable vise.

"Silver?" Danny eyed Colton's hand on her wrist as he stepped onto the dock and tied off the boat. "Everything okay here?"

Colton aimed a warning look her way. It

wasn't necessary. She hadn't forgotten his vow to arrest her if she told any civilians that he was a police officer. And even though he'd shown her no ID to prove his claim, the deputy who'd interviewed her back at the south dock had assured her—in answer to her whispered question—that Colton was definitely a Collier County deputy. Which meant his threat to arrest her was probably quite real.

She forced a smile, appreciating that the boat captain was always so nice to her, even though they'd only met a few months ago when Buddy hired him for his latest venture. "No worries, Danny. Colton is…an old friend. Everything's fine." She leaned against Colton and patted his chest when she would rather have punched him.

He played along, letting her wrist go and anchoring his arm around her shoulders, pulling her close and *very* tightly against him. "We have a lot of catching up to do."

She subtly pressed the heel of her sneaker on top of the toe of his left boot and shifted all her weight onto it while smiling at Danny as if nothing were going on. Colton grunted and eased the pressure of his arm around her. She rewarded him by moving her foot.

Danny's eyebrows climbed into his hairline. "Oh, okay. I didn't know." He slowly grinned and gave Silver a wink. "I thought there might be something going on between you two. You were whispering quite a bit on the boat earlier. Y'all have fun, um, catching up." He winked again and tipped his baseball cap. Then he headed into the little shack at the entrance to the dock, probably to lock up for the day, since the other boats were already tied up, having long ago ended their tours.

Silver stared at the closed door. Great. Danny had obviously jumped to the conclusion that she and Colton were lovers. By tomorrow the whole town would think the same thing. But what was the alternative? Telling him the truth? That wouldn't do.

"Come on." Colton grabbed her hand and

tugged her away from the building. They headed through the edge of the woods and a few minutes later emerged onto the street near the church.

After being towed along like a child's toy, Silver couldn't stand it anymore. She stopped and pushed at his hand. "Let me go. I'm not yours to pull around and manhandle no matter what threats you throw around."

He immediately dropped her hand and faced her. "Are you going to try to run away again?"

"Again? I never tried to run away."

"Oh? When you hightailed it out of the restaurant this morning, you weren't trying to get away from me?"

"I, uh, needed to talk to Buddy."

"Right. And you wanted to get on a different boat than me."

She frowned at him. "So? It's not like we knew each other."

"We know each other now. And you still tried to hop out of the boat and take off before I could catch up. If you don't like me, that's one thing. You're entitled. But let's set the record straight between us. I'm a police officer and I believe you know something about that attempted robbery today, among other things. You may have been interviewed once already, but you're about to be interviewed again. By me. And you'd better not lie anymore. I won't stand for it." He leaned down toward her, obviously using his size to try to intimidate her.

And it was working, but not the way he thought. Instead of scaring her, he was pissing her off.

"We also need to discuss that lovely blue vase sitting behind the desk at your inn," he continued, oblivious of the war going on inside her. "Because you and I both know you didn't buy it, not the honest way at least."

Shoot. "I don't know what you're talking about."

"What we're talking about is you receiving stolen property. And make no mistake, that vase is definitely stolen. That's just a fact. The who and why are what I'm going to find out. If you don't want me holding your hand, then you'd better not do anything to make me think you're trying to get away. One wrong step and I'll slap a pair of handcuffs on you."

"Oh, good grief. That's quite enough with the caveman routine." She put her hands on her hips. "If you're going to make threats, at least make ones I'll believe. Taking out handcuffs would ruin your plan to not let anyone else know your—" she did air quotes "—*super-secret* occupation. After all, we're on a public street. Someone is bound to look out a window and notice."

"You'd make a lousy cop."

She blinked up at him, thrown off by the amusement in his voice and the sudden change of subject. "What are you talking about?"

He waved toward the other businesses up the street. "You're not very observant. No one has to look out any windows when they're standing in the open watching us, and talking about us."

She looked up the street, then gasped and pressed her hand to her chest. Danny must have circled around them through the woods and had already blabbed his gossip. And his timing couldn't be worse—after rush hour, when most of the residents were back in town and doing their evening shopping.

Half the businesses had people out on the boardwalk in front, chatting with one another and not trying all that successfully to pretend that they weren't watching her and Colton. The grins and hands held over their mouths as they glanced at the two of them were a dead giveaway. As was the fact that Danny stood in the middle of one of those groups looking embarrassed when his gaze caught hers.

"I'm going to kill Danny Thompson," she muttered.

"I'll keep that in mind if something happens to him." Colton's mouth twitched suspiciously.

"Don't you dare laugh at me."

He cleared his throat. "It was the furthest thing from my mind."

She crossed her arms and gave him a smug look. "Well, one good thing has come out of this. You definitely won't be pulling out your handcuffs. Everyone will know you're a cop. Your cover would be blown."

"Honey, if I cuff you right now, I'll throw in a kiss and put you over my shoulder. My hand on your pretty little bottom will convince everyone those handcuffs have nothing to do with my occupation and everything to do with our relationship. They'll think we're into kink."

She pressed her hand against her mouth, her face warming more from his "bottom" comment than from the one about "kink."

He grinned, enjoying her discomfort far too much. "Want me to prove it?" He reached behind him as if to pull out the promised handcuffs.

"Don't you dare," she whispered harshly.

He laughed and held his hand out for hers, waiting expectantly.

She slapped her hand in his, forcing a smile that was more a baring of her teeth. "Don't expect me to hold your hand once we're inside the inn."

His smile faded and he pulled her hand to his chest, clasping it over his heart in a gesture obviously designed for their audience but that had her suddenly feeling...unfocused.

"All I plan to do once we get there is talk," he assured her. "Promise."

The kindness in his eyes, in his voice, was as unexpected as it was confusing. It was as if he realized how embarrassed she was and he felt bad about it. Maybe the show he was putting on really was just to keep his cover from being blown, and not to humiliate her.

And if she was being honest with herself, this predicament really was her fault. She never should have put her hand on Colton's rather impressively muscled chest that his snug

T-shirt did nothing to conceal and told Danny they were old friends. She should have come up with a better story than that. Colton was simply continuing the fiction that she'd created.

Dang, she hated that she couldn't be mad at him about that.

She turned toward the B and B, forcing him to lower her hand or wrench her shoulder from its socket. And as she strode toward the steps with him practically glued to her side, it occurred to her that heading into the B and B would give the gossips even more fodder. But the alternative was to head uptown and face everyone's questions.

The inn was the safer choice.

She pushed the front door open and stepped inside.

He gave her a disapproving look. "You should keep that door locked when you're not here."

"Why? Everyone knows everyone around here. We're all a big family."

"Which family member pointed the gun at us when we were on the airboat?"

She hesitated, then continued toward the great room to the right of the stairs. "I already told you that I don't know who the gunman was. And, honestly, I don't see what else you could possibly ask me that I didn't already answer when that other detective interviewed me. As I explained to him, I don't—"

"Where's the vase?"

"What?" She turned around.

He stood in front of the registration desk and gestured toward the middle cubby where the gorgeous blue vase had sat this morning. But now the spot was empty. And there was only one person she could think of who'd have taken it. *Eddie.* Probably to protect her in case the police went to her inn to question her after the botched holdup attempt.

"Did you call someone and tell them to hide it?" he asked.

"Of course not. Why would I? Assuming I

could even get a call to work around here. Trust me, this inn is right in the middle of an electronics dead zone."

"Maybe you called from the south dock, after you found out that I was a cop, and you remembered my interest in that vase. You were worried that you'd get into trouble for accepting stolen property. So you asked a friend to move it somewhere else."

She crossed her arms. "Or maybe, like you said, I should have kept my front door locked."

His mouth twitched. "I guess I deserved that one."

The man really shouldn't smile like that. It made her notice those incredible blue eyes again and it was killing her concentration.

"What does a vase that may or may not be stolen have to do with you interviewing me about the gunman anyway?"

He leaned against the registration desk and crossed his long legs at the ankles. "Fair question. How about we start over? I'm Collier

County Deputy Colton Graham. I'm working undercover to bring down a burglary ring that's been operating in Naples for the past six months. This morning I followed one of the suspects here to Mystic Glades. The same man who held up that blue vase in front of your inn and then went inside—Eddie Rafferty. The same man who I believe pointed a gun at a boat full of people this morning when he tried to rob them, when he tried to rob you and me. Does that clear it up?"

She raised her chin a notch. "I suppose it does. What's *clear* is that you've made a terrible mistake. The vase you believe to be stolen obviously looks like some other vase. You've confused the two."

"Oh, I have, have I?"

"You most certainly have. And since I can't tell you who that gunman was, there's no point in even continuing this conversation."

"Can't? Or won't?"

She let out an impatient breath. "In case

you've forgotten, I have a grand opening tomorrow. And although most everything is ready, I'd like to take advantage of the last few hours of daylight that we have left to double-check all the rooms and menus. And I also need to confirm that my two helpers are still set to arrive in the morning. Which means I have to run an errand, to go visit them."

"Them? Just who are these helpers?"

"Not that you really need to know, but I've hired a friend's daughter, Tippy, to help me run the inn all summer, starting tomorrow. The work will look good on her résumé, since she's pursuing a degree in hospitality."

"You said *them*. Who else is coming?"

"Her boyfriend, Jenks. He'll do the chores around here." She waved her hand impatiently. "None of that matters. Like I said, I need to make sure everything is set. You're of course welcome to stay in your room, free of charge, as long as you don't interfere with my work. It's the least I can do for a police officer. I'll cancel the charge against your credit card."

"Very kind of you," he said, his voice dry.

"If that's all, then, I'll just go—"

"There was a small painting displayed here earlier. It's missing, too." He gestured toward the wall of cubbies behind the registration desk.

She noted the empty square and let out a cry of dismay. "That was one of my favorite pieces."

"Eddie sold you that one, too, huh?"

Her stomach sank with dread. No, he hadn't *sold* it to her. "Why did you remember that particular painting?" she whispered.

"You know why." His voice was soft this time, kind even, without its accusatory edge. As if he realized she'd just had a shock, even if he didn't understand why.

She could do without his pity. She certainly didn't deserve it. *Stupid, stupid, stupid.* How could she have been so gullible? Even though she considered herself a temporary caretaker of the vase and other items that Eddie had sold her, she'd never once suspected that the painting was stolen, too.

It had been a gift, no money exchanged between them. He'd brought it to her after she helped him study for an algebra final exam. He'd been close to tears, telling her he wouldn't have graduated if she hadn't helped him. The painting was his way of saying thank-you and had supposedly been purchased with money from mowing lawns and other odd jobs he'd worked last summer. She'd treasured it, not for its beauty, but for the sentiment behind it. And now to find out that it was just like everything else he'd brought broke her heart.

She sank onto the nearest chair, a ladder-back she'd restrung herself, after painting the wood a cozy, happy yellow. But even her favorite chair couldn't make her smile now.

A few weeks ago, she'd thought she had everything under control. Things were going as planned. And she'd believed—foolishly, she now realized—that she could cover for Eddie, at least until she managed to extricate him from the mire he was caught up in. And then, once that was taken care of, she'd planned to have a heart-to-heart talk with him and insist all the stolen items be returned. She'd be his advocate in court. She'd explain everything that had been going on in the hopes that the court would be understanding and would be lenient with him. She'd hoped to *save* him. But now, thanks to this irritating, nosy cop, it was clear that she might have done more harm than good.

Colton sighed and crouched down in front of her, his face a study in compassion. He took her hands between his, surprising her so much that she didn't try to pull back. She stared into his cobalt-blue eyes and was rather shocked at the zing of awareness that shot through her. Before now she'd thought of him only as a potential model for one of her projects, or the irritating police officer who was interfering with her life. But now, seeing that gentle, concerned look on his face, with those incredible eyes seeming to delve into her very soul, she was noticing him in an entirely different way. A way that made her body melt from the inside out.

Good grief. She was attracted to him.

She yanked her hands from his and pressed back against the chair. This was even more of a disaster than she'd feared. There was no room, and no time in her life for a relationship. Not now. And certainly not with a man who was, in many ways, her enemy.

He sighed and stood, looking mildly disappointed in her. And for some reason, that stung.

"We can rule out that a stranger came in here and robbed you," he said, "unlocked door or not. Whoever took the vase and that painting was specifically here for those items."

"Why do you say that?"

"If a typical burglar had come in here, he wouldn't have left behind the other valuables." He waved toward the network of shelves.

Not sure what he was talking about, she looked at the mixture of plants, books and other knickknacks decorating each cubby. "I don't understand what you mean. Everything of value *was* taken."

He gave her an incredulous look and pointed at a small five-by-seven painting on the third shelf down. "That has to be worth several hundred dollars." He pointed to another one on the far right. "And that one? I can't even guess. But I've had a crash course in art valuation on various assignments this past year and I know that painting would fetch an exorbitant price at auction."

She blinked, wondering just what he meant by exorbitant. "You think those pieces are... valuable?"

"Of course." He searched her gaze. "You don't?"

Her face flushed with heat and she shrugged. "I suppose so. Maybe." Since she was the one who'd created those particular pieces to decorate the inn, she'd never thought about their monetary value. It was...nice, unexpected...

to have someone besides her look at them and think they held more than just sentimental value. Although art, and making art, had always been important to her, she'd never felt confident enough to try to sell any of her pieces. They never seemed good enough.

His look turned suspicious, as if he thought she was lying about the paintings. Maybe he believed they were stolen, too, but that they hadn't popped onto his radar yet. She'd like to put his mind at ease, but telling him that he'd just complimented her own work felt far too…intimate… to share with him after all the lies she'd told. And the threats he'd made.

Intimate? Who was she kidding? She'd asked him to pose nude for her. It didn't get much more intimate than that. But that was all about her art. Now, knowing he was a cop and that she'd asked him to pose for her, she was mortified.

He stepped closer to study one of her canvases, a depiction of the Glades at dawn, with fields of golden saw grass bending in the breeze while a whooping crane searched for its next meal. Colton was probably looking for the artist's signature to see if it was listed with the other stolen goods he was investigating. Before he could find her initials hidden in the intricate details of a wildflower near the bottom right corner, she rose from her chair, drawing his attention.

"Are we finished here?" she asked.

"Are you ready to finally tell the truth?"

If only it were that simple. But the truth would bring more policemen, scouring through the woods, putting all the residents on high alert. And *that* would be a disaster.

"What else do you want to know?" she asked, beginning to fear that this was a losing battle. The man just didn't know when to quit.

"Where's Eddie Rafferty?"

Hopefully lying low, staying out of harm's way until she could get to him.

"I don't know."

"And you wouldn't tell me if you did, would you?"

She braced her hand on the edge of the registration desk, her fingers curling against the wood. "He's not the bad person that you think he is. He's just a kid—"

"He's *eighteen*, legally an adult. Old enough to vote, old enough to die for his country. Which means he's plenty old enough to know right from wrong, and he should pay the consequences for the choices he's made. Where is he?"

She wasn't sure, but she knew who his friends were. And even though *Eddie* didn't know that she knew, she also knew his favorite hiding places. Finding him wouldn't be all that difficult. And she *needed* to find him. Because that attempted holdup had changed everything. She'd bring him into the police station herself if she could just get this relentless detective to give her a break so she could slip away and bring Eddie in *safely*.

"Silver, this is your chance to do the right thing. Tell me where he is."

Again, his voice was soft, understanding. Too bad they were on opposite sides. He was exactly the sort of man she could like, respect, admire. But his timing couldn't be worse.

"And if I don't *do the right thing*, you're going to arrest me?"

He frowned, his dark eyebrows lowering. "I don't want to. But if you force my hand, I will."

She considered her options, her plans. But there was really only one option that she could think of that would end this stalemate without sacrificing Eddie. Even if it meant sacrificing the inn, and everything that she'd worked for.

She held her hands out, palms up. "I guess I'm forcing your hand."

Chapter Six

"What the Fourth of July were you thinking, Detective?"

Colton would have laughed at his boss's die-hard commitment to avoid cursing, but his ears were ringing from the shouting. He belatedly wished he *hadn't* closed the office door. Then maybe some of the sound waves would have swept through the open doorway into the squad room, reducing the shouts to a bearable decibel level. Then again, with the door *open*, what few peers of his were still around, owing to the late hour, would hear the dressing-down he was being given. So maybe the closed door was a good thing. It was a toss-up.

He rested his forearms on his knees and leaned forward in his chair. Drew glared at him from behind his desk, his face so red he looked as if he was about to have a stroke. Colton was doing his best to calm him down, but nothing he'd said so far was working. He supposed he was just going to have to weather the storm.

"What else was I supposed to do?" he said, keeping his voice as calm and nonconfrontational as possible. "She basically told me to arrest her."

"Well, I wouldn't have expected you to actually do it." Drew shoved a folder out of his way, frowned, then picked it up and put it on a stack of folders, carefully aligning all the edges.

Again, Colton wanted to laugh. Or knock the stack askew just to see Drew straighten it again. But he rather enjoyed his job—most of the time—and didn't relish the idea of being fired.

"I can just see this in social media," Drew practically growled. "Collier County Deputy Manhandles Woman Who Witnessed Attempted Holdup."

"*Witnessed*, my…" His boss's warning glare made Colton stop before he broke the golden no-cursing rule that Drew had instituted after taking over the leadership from the former lieutenant. Trying to clean up the department's poor image in the press was a worthy goal, certainly. But the no cursing, even when civilians weren't present, seemed a bit extreme—especially to guys like Colton who spent much of their time undercover. Criminals didn't go around saying *darn* and *shoot*, and neither did Colton when he was pretending to be one of them. Which just made it all that much harder when he was in the office. Like now.

He drew a bracing breath and tried again. "What I'm saying is that Miss Westbrook isn't simply a witness. And you know it. She's a part of whatever's going on in Mystic Glades."

Drew flattened his palms on the desk. "You do realize that any rent-by-the-hour attorney will get her out within minutes. And they'll just make us look heavy-handed to the press. Officer Scott told me she's already contacted a lawyer. Heck, he's probably already in the interrogation room with her by now. We're going to have our heads handed to us on a platter."

Colton rose to his feet. There was only so much he could take, and he'd about reached his limit. "Drew—"

"Don't call me that. I'm too ticked off to be your friend right now."

"Fine, *Lieutenant Shlafer*. But keep in mind that I've been deep undercover on this case for months. Rafferty is the closest to a true lead that I've gotten. And I don't know where he is. And now he's pulled a gun on someone, graduating from burglary to armed robbery. In case you haven't noticed, this is escalating, fast. Someone's going to get hurt or killed if I don't get a jump on this. And right now my only chance is to interrogate and intimidate his guardian angel into spilling the beans on him. I don't know about you, but I don't want to sit around on my…butt…waiting for something worse to happen. What if I hadn't been on that boat? What if that kid hadn't gotten scared off? Someone could have been killed."

A knock sounded on the door.

Drew glared at Colton, letting him know just what he thought of his little speech. "Come in."

The door opened and one of the uniformed officers stepped in. "Miss Westbrook's lawyer spoke to the judge and the charges were dropped."

"Perfect," Drew muttered. "Now we look even more inept. All right. Put the paperwork through to release her."

"Already done."

Drew gave Colton a hard look. "At least someone around here is efficient and on the ball."

Colton gave him the best comeback he could think of. He smiled.

Drew narrowed his eyes.

"Lieutenant?" the officer at the door called out again.

"What?" Drew yelled, then reddened. He cleared his throat. "Sorry. What else can I help you with?"

"Miss Westbrook wants to speak to you before she leaves."

"Well, of course she does. And I'll just bet her lawyer tags along with her, so they can tell us together that they're suing for false arrest."

Colton couldn't help it. He rolled his eyes.

Drew jabbed his finger in the air, pointing at him. "As for you, Detective. I'm going to—"

"Sir," the officer called out again. "Miss Westbrook is here, right now, to see you."

"All right, all right." Drew pulled on his suit jacket with quick, jerky movements. "Send her in."

The officer moved back and Silver stepped through the doorway.

Colton and Drew rose to their feet just as two men in dark suits stepped in behind Silver.

"She needed two lawyers?" Colton grumbled beneath his breath.

He must not have been as quiet as he'd thought, because one of the men gave him a sharp look.

"No," the man said, directing his comment to Colton. "She only has one lawyer—Mr. Stanton." He waved toward the other man.

"Then who are you?" Colton asked.

"He's my boss," Silver said, drawing everyone's attention back to her. "Lieutenant Shlafer, Detective Graham, meet Special Agent Eduardo Garcia. DEA."

EVERYONE STARTED TALKING at once.

Silver tried to intervene, but her boss, Colton's boss, and even the lawyer her boss had brought with him to supposedly ensure cooperation and make sure any charges against her were dropped, were all so busy arguing with one another that she couldn't get their attention.

"I think this is where the art of a stealthy re-treat comes in," Colton whispered as he passed by her on his way to the door. He held it open in invitation.

After casting another irritated look at the other men who were steadfastly ignoring her, even though this whole situation was *about* her, she followed Colton into the squad room.

He led her to an empty desk well away from the few desks that still had detectives on phones or typing up reports. Most of the room was de-serted, probably because it was well after seven in the evening and everyone else had gone home to their families.

Since she'd been sitting for over two hours—counting the trip from Mystic Glades, hand-cuffed, in Colton's car—she turned down his offer of a seat and chose instead to lean back against the desk.

He joined her, leaning back beside her, arms crossed and his long legs spread out in front of him. They both stared at the far wall for a minute, a depressing gray decorated with an even more depressing collection of plaques. Above them were two simple, but poignant words. *Our Fallen.* She shivered and rubbed her hands up and down her arms.

"So," Colton finally said. "DEA, huh?"

"Yep."

"How long?"

"Eight years. What about you?"

He thumped his fingers against the edge of the desk. "About the same, I reckon, come October."

The silence stretched out between them again. Or, rather, it would have been silent if it weren't for the thankfully muted sound of yelling coming through the walls of Lieutenant Shlafer's office behind them. It sounded like a war going on.

"Don't let it bother you," Colton said, jerking his head toward the office. "They're probably trying to figure out whose is bigger."

"Is that supposed to be funny?"

He sighed. "Apparently not. I was just trying to cut through some of the tension in here. You want a soda or something?"

She shook her head. "No, but feel free to leave. I don't need a babysitter."

"Yeah. I kind of figured that once you introduced your boss. DEA, huh? Why didn't you tell me?"

"I was undercover, just like you."

"But after you found out that I was a cop, you should have told me."

"Really? Just like that, I should have trusted you?"

"Of course."

She glanced around the room to make sure no one was paying them any attention before she replied, "Tell me, Detective."

"Call me Colton. I've been calling you Silver all this time. The least you can do is use my first name, too, so I don't feel like quite as much of an idiot for being in the dark."

She couldn't help smiling at that. He was obviously feeling put out that he hadn't guessed she was in law enforcement. "All right. Colton. If you'd spent months deep undercover and you met an undercover police officer who could *blow* your cover if he didn't believe your story, would you have leveled with him and risked everything?"

"No way."

"Thank you."

He frowned. "Okay, so you moved to Mystic Glades, what, a few months ago?"

"Six."

"Only six?"

"Yep. Why does that surprise you?"

He tapped the desk again. "In that bar, you seemed pretty cozy with everyone, like you belonged there. And you knew all about that Freddie woman and the guy she liked."

"Labron. And that's because I do belong there. It's where I grew up. I left to go to college, and then to start my career. Mostly I worked out of the office down in the Keys. But I always went back every summer, kept up on everything going on. Since I couldn't risk word getting out that I was DEA since I mostly work undercover, I told everyone I paid the bills with my art. They always knew me as that flighty daydreamer who'd rather paint than go shoe shopping anyway." She shrugged. "The ruse worked. And when tourism finally came to Mystic Glades, I thought it was a sign that it was finally time to take all the money I'd saved over the years and chase my dream."

"The bed-and-breakfast? It's your dream?"

She nodded. "I put in notice at my job and hired a contractor to start the work on that plot of land my grandfather had passed down to me."

"You said you put in notice. Obviously you didn't end up quitting. What happened?"

"Eddie Rafferty."

He gave her a curious look. "What do you mean?"

She tried not to let it distract her that his shoulder kept brushing against hers whenever he talked, or that he smelled so clean and masculine—probably his soap. Whether they'd said it out loud or not, the minute he found out that she was a fellow law-enforcement officer, his demeanor toward her had changed. He was now treating her like an equal, a comrade in arms.

And without the hostility bubbling between them, she could finally let her guard down. But that seemed to have been a green light for her hormones, too. Because she kept getting distracted by little things about him—like the sexy rumble of his deep voice in his chest, or the way he'd held the door open for her earlier, or that he was asking her questions instead of making more accusations. He was all good *hot* cop now. And she was more than relieved to say a permanent goodbye to *bad* cop.

"Silver? You were going to explain about Rafferty?"

She looked away, focusing on a painting—a poster, really—hanging on another wall, just outside of a conference room. It wasn't to her taste. The colors were too muted. But she couldn't seem to pull a coherent thought together when he turned the full attention of those gorgeous baby blues her way.

"Eddie was busing tables at Gators and Taters last summer when I was staying with some friends who run the Moon and Star."

"Moon and Star? I think I remember that. It's across the street from Callahan's?"

She nodded. "Faye Star, well, Faye *Young* now that she and Jake got married, owns the shop. It's a mystical kind of thing with potions, fragrances, even some clothing you wouldn't find anywhere else." She waved her hand in the air. "Anyway, I was staying in their guest room above the shop while on vacation. When I was having lunch at G&T, I met Eddie. I guess I… noticed a kindred spirit, saw the way others treated him, like he was invisible. Like just because he didn't have a family, and didn't fit in, that he wasn't worthy of their time. So I made time, made the effort to offer him friendship. I even helped him with his homework."

She could feel his stare, but she didn't turn to face him.

"Kindred spirit," he said. "Because you focus so much on your art? Because people can't understand your world so they don't go out of their way to welcome you into their circles?"

This time, she *did* look at him. "Most people would say I'm *unfocused.*"

"They'd be wrong. I've always thought of artists as having a sixth sense, the ability to see another dimension, another plane of existence that others don't. That ability, to see, *really* see, and to find joy in everything and everyone around you is your superpower, while the rest of us are handicapped."

She blinked back the unexpected hot burn of tears at the backs of her eyes. "What an amazing thing to say."

"Yeah, well." He cleared his throat, suddenly

looking uncomfortable. "Just calling it like I see it."

"You really do have a sister who's an artist, don't you?"

"Yep."

"And she lives in Atlanta?"

"Right again. I'm not the one who told a passel of lies since meeting you. Most of what I said was the truth."

"Ouch." Those tears weren't burning to be shed anymore.

He lightly bumped her shoulder with his in a show of camaraderie. "No worries. I get it. I'd have done the same thing. To some extent."

A moment of awkward silence passed between them. She didn't need him to tell her exactly how she'd bungled her job. She was well aware of that.

"Finish your story," he said. "How did meeting Eddie change your plans to quit the DEA?"

"I saw him arguing at the edge of the woods with a couple of other guys—one of his foster brothers—Charlie Tate—who's Eddie's age, and Ron Dukes, a troublemaker in his midtwenties who has no business hanging out with high school kids. And their argument didn't strike me as typical, either. They were far too serious, and they kept glancing around, like they were looking for someone, or maybe worried that someone might see them. A few seconds later, Ron led the other two of them into the woods."

He stiffened beside her. "You followed them?"

"I did."

"Even though your instincts told you that something was off?"

She crossed her arms. "It's not like I was out of my element. I know every inch of Mystic Glades. And I'm an officer of the law. It's my job to investigate things that don't look right."

"Tell me you at least had your sidearm."

"Are you going to let me finish this or not?"

He crossed his arms in an echo of her pose and gave her a curt nod.

"Okay, no, I didn't have my gun with me. But it was because I was on vacation, in my hometown. I didn't have any reason to expect something like that would happen."

"Something like what, exactly?"

"I followed Ron, Charlie and Eddie about a mile in. Then Ron pulled a brick of cocaine out of a hollowed-out tree."

He cursed beneath his breath.

"No one got hurt," she said, knowing he was still upset that she hadn't had her gun with her that day. "I knew a bad scene when I saw it. I didn't confront any of them. Instead, I backtracked to town and then hightailed it out of the Glades so I could call my boss."

"You should always, always, have your sidearm. Hell, I even take mine into the bathroom. And I sleep with it under my pillow. Even when I'm undercover I carry a gun. Hell, especially undercover. You should, too."

"Yeah, well. Maybe I just suck at being a cop." She echoed his earlier words back at him.

"No. You don't suck at being a cop. You're just too close to this, because you know Eddie, and Mystic Glades is your hometown. Your boss thought that would be an asset after you told him about that kilo, didn't he?" He didn't wait for her response. "He sent you in there to track down the supply of drugs. And then, what, you discovered Eddie was in deeper than you thought? And you found out he was involved in the burglary ring, too?"

She pursed her lips and stared at the opposite wall again.

"You don't have to answer," he said. "I can guess the rest, based on my own observations from earlier today. Instead of hauling Eddie in and getting him to roll on his friends, you covered for him and tried to figure out how to keep him out of jail and still catch the bad guys. But that's where you went wrong. Because Eddie is one of those bad guys. You let your friendship with him cloud your judgment. That's why you lied to me today about the holdup."

The more he spoke, the angrier he sounded. It was as if all the pieces were falling into place and destroying any fellow law-enforcement empathy he'd had for her just moments ago.

She didn't try to defend herself. What would be the point? Everything he was saying was true. She'd screwed up.

"You weren't worried that I'd blow your cover like you probably told your boss," Colton continued, sounding disgusted. "You were worried that if you told me the truth, I'd tell you that you're too close to this. You had every opportunity to come clean. When the other officers interviewed you outside Mystic Glades, where we all had cell phone coverage and could have verified your story with one call to the DEA, you continued to lie. And the *reason* that you lied wasn't so you could protect your case. The reason you lied was to protect Eddie Rafferty. Everything that you've done was to keep me from hauling that kid to jail. Admit it."

She stared into a pair of stormy blue eyes that

had darkened with anger, not sure what to say, or even whether she *should* say anything. After experiencing his support, and his thoughtful insight into something she'd struggled with all her life—the way she viewed the world through her artist's lens—she found it so much worse now to be the object of such hostility from him. As if she'd discovered a friend, or something… deeper, only to have it whisked away.

"Is all of that true, Agent Westbrook?" a voice demanded.

Her heart stuttered in her chest as she turned to see her boss standing beside a stunned-looking Lieutenant Shlafer. There could be no doubt. They'd heard every word, every accusation that Colton had just made. But what made her humiliation worse was that Colton had to have known they were standing there. He'd been half turned toward her, and her back had been to Shlafer's office. He'd known they were there, the whole time, and he'd kept going, spouting off things that could very well destroy her career.

"Well?" Garcia demanded, his voice so sharp it could have cut glass.

She pushed away from the desk and stood ramrod straight, refusing to look at Colton. She fervently hoped that after today, she'd never have to see him again.

"I was trying to figure out the best way to extricate Rafferty from the trouble he was in, yes. But, as we previously discussed, I was also using him and his contacts to discover who was heading up the drug-running operation, and how they were bringing the drugs in and out of the Everglades."

"Conference. Now." Garcia whirled around and marched back toward Shlafer's office.

Colton raised his hand toward her, regret mirrored in the tiny lines of tension around the corners of his eyes. "Silver, I'm sorry. I didn't mean to—"

She pushed his hand away and straightened

her shoulders. "My *name* is Special Agent West-brook." After making a wide berth around him, she followed her boss into the office and shut the door.

Colton dropped his hand to his side, hating that he'd caused that hurt that had flashed across Silver's face after his tirade. His anger had bled out as soon as he saw that look and realized what he'd done. But he'd been so upset that she'd made so many poor choices, mainly because she could have gotten herself hurt, or worse. As to *why* the idea of her getting hurt bothered him so much, well, he didn't even want to go there. It didn't make sense that he'd care so much, not after knowing her for less than a day.

Now who was losing focus?

He shook his head in disgust. "I made a royal mess out of that."

"Yeah, you did," Drew said. "But you were right. And you didn't say anything that her boss didn't already guess. He was planning on confronting her after we shared everything about our cases."

"Shared?" Colton snorted. "Is that what you call all that yelling?" He glanced around. "And what did you do with the lawyer? Is he back in your office?"

Drew grinned. "We gave him a headache. I think he went downstairs for an aspirin." He plopped down in the chair that Silver had refused earlier. "Special Agent Garcia has been worried about her working alone on this case but wasn't sure how to help her without blowing her cover. People in the Glades aren't quick to trust outsiders."

"So what's he going to do now?"

"Pull her. He'll send a team into the marsh to see if they can salvage any evidence, maybe get lucky. But most likely they'll have to start a new investigation to stop the flow of drugs moving through there, from outside of Mystic Glades."

"That's a shame. From what she said, she was close to a break in the case."

"You thought the same thing, and look where we are on that."

He winced. "Point taken. What do you want me to do? Find Rafferty and bring him in?"

"I think that's about the only thing we *can* do at this point. Cut our losses. We'll coordinate with Garcia, help him salvage as much as possible from Westbrook's investigation. Then we all start over." He pushed the chair back from the desk and stood.

"All right," Colton said. "The kid's gone to ground right now. I think we should give him a couple of days to start feeling secure before we go looking for him. Then I'll get a couple of guys to go with me up through the canals and we'll sneak in the back way. We'll catch him as soon as he pops his head up somewhere."

Drew nodded. "Sounds like a good plan. I'll see if Garcia wants to—"

"Lieutenant." Another detective several desks away held up one of the landline phones. "There's a call for you, from the Miccosukee."

"Miccosukee? Their resort's almost two hours away. Why aren't they calling Broward County or Miami-Dade if they need help?"

"Not the resort. Alligator Alley. The Miccosukee police out on their section of I-75 said they've had some kind of incident that you need to know about."

Drew took the call. From the way his jaw tightened, Colton knew the news was bad. The detective who'd notified him about the call grabbed a piece of paper off the printer on his desk and handed that to Drew as well. The lieutenant read it while he spoke on the phone, then shook his head and tucked the paper into his suit jacket pocket. By the time Drew ended the call, Silver and her boss had finished their meeting and joined Colton in front of the desk.

Silver's face was pale and she wouldn't meet Colton's gaze. He was about to demand that Garcia tell him what he'd said to her when Drew joined them. He nodded at Silver and Garcia, before his weary gaze met Colton's.

"What happened?" Colton asked.

"The Miccosukee police had heard about the attempted holdup earlier and that we were interested in interviewing Rafferty." He glanced at Silver before continuing. "There was a 911 call a few hours ago around mile marker fifty-two on I-75, in their jurisdiction, and they just briefed me on their initial findings." He cleared his throat and looked at Silver again.

She sucked in a breath and fisted her hands at her sides.

"Please," she said, her voice so tight and hoarse that she couldn't finish her sentence.

Garcia gave her an odd look, as if he didn't understand what the rest of them had already guessed.

Colton circled around him and stood behind Silver. He put his hands lightly on her shoulders, as a show of support and to let her know that even if her boss was being a jerk, she wasn't in this alone. Instead of pushing him away, as he'd half feared, she took the support he offered and subtly shifted so that her back was pressed against his chest. Colton nodded at Drew to continue.

His face was a mask of misery and sympathy as he broke the news. "I'm sorry, Agent Westbrook. Eddie Rafferty is dead."

Her body started to shake and she wobbled against him as if she was about to collapse.

Colton reacted on instinct, wrapping his arms around her waist and holding her tight. He didn't care one whit that Garcia frowned at him or that Drew raised an eyebrow. She'd fought for that kid, had allowed herself to be arrested and risked losing her inn for him. Maybe Colton didn't agree with her choices, but he admired her just the same for fighting for a troubled young man whom everyone else had thrown away—including Colton. He couldn't help feeling guilty about that now.

When Silver didn't say anything, Colton asked the questions that needed to be asked, the questions that he knew she'd want the answers to, later, when she could move past her shock and process them.

"How?" he asked. "What happened?"

Drew hesitated and shot an uncertain look at Silver.

"Say it," Colton told him. "She needs to know."

Drew looked to Silver's boss for guidance, but Garcia shrugged as if he didn't have a clue how to handle Silver's silence.

"A motorist called it in a couple of hours ago," Drew said. "A body lying in the grass beside the highway. The coroner still has to perform an autopsy, of course, but the cause of death is probably internal injuries. He was beaten, and…" He looked at Silver again. "I don't think the medical details are pertinent at the moment. Suffice it to say, he was murdered. And the evidence suggests it was the primary site. He was killed right there on the side of the highway."

Silver drew a sharp breath and started pushing at Colton's arms around her waist. He let her go and she shoved away from him, wobbling like a drunk on her feet.

Colton reached for her, but she scrambled back out of his way. "Silver, let me help—"

"No, don't," she whispered, her voice full of anguish. "I have to… I need to go to the ladies' room."

The stubborn woman looked as though she was about to pass out, but Colton didn't argue. He could tell she was about to break down and she desperately wanted some privacy before that happened. "Down that hallway, first door on the right." He waved toward the right side of the room.

"Thank you," she whispered, then made her way unsteadily out of the room.

Garcia frowned after her. "She shouldn't be that upset. She's too softhearted, too weak for this job. I should have recognized that years ago. And now she's obviously crossed the line even more than I'd realized, made this personal."

Colton swore. "You do realize she knew Rafferty before your case started, right? He was in high school. A kid. She even helped him with his homework. But she still did her job, let you know that he was mixed up with a drug-running operation. And she was working to bring that operation down in spite of that personal connection to Rafferty. If she's choked up over his death, it's understandable, expected. From where I stand, you're the one with the problem. You aren't making this personal enough. You should be offering her support and understanding instead of criticizing her."

Garcia took a step toward him, his dark eyes flashing with anger. "Watch your tongue, Detective."

Colton matched his step. "Why don't you—"

"Hey, hey, hey." Drew moved between them, pushing his hands against them to keep them apart. "Back off, gentlemen. This has been a stressful day for all of us. Let's leave our opinions and our egos at the door and focus on our cases."

"What cases?" Garcia sneered. "Rafferty was the link to the robbery ring and the drug ring. There *aren't* any cases anymore. We have to start over. This is a complete cluster from beginning to end." He glared at Colton. "Since you're so cozy with Westbrook, you can give her a message for me when she comes back. She's fired."

Colton shoved Drew's hand out of his way so he could reach Garcia, but the agent whirled around and strode toward the exit.

"Let it go," Drew ordered.

"He's a colossal jerk who doesn't even support his own agents," Colton ground out.

"Agreed. But it's his call. She'd given notice that she was quitting after this case anyway. It's not like he destroyed her career."

"Maybe not, but once she works through her grief, she'll want to catch Eddie's killer. And without the DEA's support, she's lost her vehicle for doing that. You know good and well the Miccosukee police aren't going to know what to do with this one. And we sure don't want them trouncing over our burglary ring while trying to solve the murder. It's part of our case. We should take it and find Eddie's killer. And if there are drugs flowing through Mystic Glades, we can't turn a blind eye just because Garcia does. Someone needs to stop it."

"I'm well aware of that. But if this wasn't political before, it just got political. I'll have to smooth Garcia's ruffled feathers and see if we can't come up with a joint plan, maybe even a task force. Obviously if Rafferty was involved in both cases, it makes sense to work together. It's a pretty safe bet that the guy at the top is running both the drugs and the burglary ring. I'll have to think on this and figure out how to handle it without putting my job on the line. First things first, we need to notify Rafferty's family."

"He didn't have a family. He was in the foster system, never adopted."

"Oh, man. Poor kid."

"Yeah. Poor kid." Colton shook his head. "From what I can tell, Silver's all he had. But I can ask her about it. We can do the notification together if there's anyone to notify. Or I can do it alone once I get the details from her."

"Works for me." Drew pulled the piece of paper out of his suit jacket pocket that the other detective had given him while he was on the phone. "I was going to tell the others about this, but obviously Miss Westbrook is in no shape to read it right now."

"What is it?"

"A copy of a letter from Rafferty, addressed to Miss Westbrook. The original was found in his jeans pocket in an envelope, so the responding officer emailed us a picture of it that he took with his phone. Looks like Eddie had planned on mailing it to her when he got to wherever he was going. I assume he avoided text or email, since the coverage is unreliable in Mystic Glades. Unfortunately he never got the chance to send it." He handed it to Colton.

"Take her home. Watch over her for a few days and then check back in with me. I'll put you on paid administrative leave until I get together with Garcia and we decide where to go from here. If he won't do what he should—support his agent when she's in crisis—then we'll have to do his damn job for him."

Colton stared in shock at his boss. "Did you just say—"

"Do you like your job, Detective?" Drew practically growled.

He choked back a laugh. "Yes, sir. I do. Which means I never heard you break your own cursing rule."

"Good answer." Drew headed toward his office.

Chapter Seven

Colton glanced at Silver in the passenger seat of his Mustang as he drove under the archway into Mystic Glades. But she was just as silent, just as withdrawn as she'd been since Drew announced that Eddie was dead. She hadn't even reacted when Colton told her that her boss had fired her.

She was definitely in shock, and probably blaming herself, second-guessing everything and replaying the investigation over and over in her mind to see if she could have done something differently. He hated that she was going through this, but at least she wasn't pushing him away. No one should have to face grief like that alone.

As he pulled into a parking space in front of the B and B, he frowned at the lack of lights outside. At a minimum, the porch light should be on to help dispel the darkness. A streetlight would be better, something that would cast a glow across the entire front yard, especially since the inn was a bit isolated from the other businesses. There were streetlights farther up the street, but they stopped short of the B and B.

It was only a little past ten, but with all the businesses closed except for Callahan's Watering Hole, which was a good distance away, it seemed even later. And too quiet. Silver's inn seemed far too vulnerable for his liking. He'd have to talk to her about the lighting and maybe even a high privacy fence, at least on the sides of the property. That would remove a burglar's ability to hide in the bushes and trees. Anyone intending harm to the inn or its inhabitants would be forced to come out on the street in full view or approach from the back. He'd take a tour of the property tomorrow in daylight and see just how bad the security setup was.

Glancing over at Silver, who seemed to be lost in her own little world at the moment looking out at the dark sky, he was glad he'd brought her home and that he'd be there tonight to watch over her. Because right now he wasn't sure she could protect herself if it came to that.

He took his pistol out of his ankle holster and slid it into his waistband so he'd have it at the ready. He'd been thinking about Eddie's murder the whole way here and had come to a conclusion. If the burglary or drug ringleader was behind Eddie's murder—which seemed the logical conclusion—then the only reason to kill Eddie and leave his body in a public place was that the killer wanted him found. Which meant the killing was a message. Eddie had to have done something that put the killer at risk, and his murder was to warn others not to do anything similar.

But the only true risk to a drug boss would be exposure to law enforcement. And since Silver was the only law-enforcement officer in Mystic Glades and she had established a friendship with Eddie, then putting those together added up to one thing—Colton was convinced that the killer knew that Silver was DEA and that Eddie was her contact. The kid might not have realized he was being used, but his "boss" would have figured it out if Eddie mentioned anything about Silver and then the boss did some research. If he had the right contacts, he might have figured out that Silver was a threat.

Which meant Colton needed to stay extra vigilant, at least for the next few days until his boss soothed Garcia and figured out a new game plan.

"Silver," he whispered, not wanting to startle her in the quiet of the car. "Hey, Silver?"

She shook herself as if waking up. "Oh. We're here. Sorry."

She popped the door, but Colton leaned across

her and pulled it shut. She looked at him in question.

He patted the gun at his waist. "I'd rather you wait until I get out and open your door. It's dark out here, and we don't know what Eddie may have told his killer, and what they may have deduced. We have to assume we're being watched. And since you don't have a gun—"

"I have a gun. Garcia gave it to me before, well, before everything went south at the station." She yanked her pant leg up to reveal an ankle holster much like his, with a Ruger 9 mm snapped into place. She let her pant leg drop. "I'm just keeping it hidden. You know, because B and B owners don't typically walk around with guns at their waists. It's bad for business."

He smiled. "You had me worried earlier. But you're going to be okay, aren't you?"

Tears suddenly brightened her eyes, but she blinked them back. "I'm okay."

"Wait here." He hated that he'd managed to bring her out of her stupor one moment and then had her ready to weep the next. She was still fragile, and he needed to keep a close eye on her. He hopped out and moved quickly around to the passenger door, keeping a watchful eye on the woods to the left and right of the property before opening her door.

A hurried walk down the path through the middle of the front lawn, with him looking left and right every few seconds, his right hand on the butt of his gun at his waist, found them at the front door.

She turned the knob, then turned it again. "I don't understand. Why won't it open?"

Colton shook the keys in his left hand. "Because I made you lock it when we left. You don't remember?" He put the key in the lock and opened the door.

"Now I remember."

She started to step inside first, but he moved past and pulled her in behind him, tucking her back against the wall as he locked the door. He flipped the entrance hall light switch and pulled out his gun, still blocking her with his body as he scanned their surroundings.

"Stay here while I do a security sweep. Stay alert. And don't hesitate to use your gun if someone other than me comes back. I'll announce myself before I step back into the foyer."

"No." She pulled her gun from its holster and held it down by her side, pointing at the floor. "We'll both clear the house."

"Silver, I don't think that's a—"

"Good idea?" she finished for him. "I'm grieving. And I feel guilty as hell for what happened to Eddie. But I'm not helpless. I'll deal with this. And just because Garcia fired me doesn't mean I'm suddenly not capable of using my training." She motioned toward the doorway to their left. "You can start with the kitchen and dining room, and circle around to the hallway that runs across the back of the house. I'll go right and clear the gathering room, the bathroom under the stairs, and circle around to the same hallway."

He agreed reluctantly, and they each headed off in a different direction. They ended up meeting halfway down the hallway she'd mentioned, after he'd cleared the two rooms.

"What else is down there?" he asked, waving toward the other end of the hall.

"Bathroom, office and a sunroom. I cleared all three."

"Does this place have a back door? I didn't see one."

"Through the sunroom. And before you ask, yes, I locked it. Let's hurry and check upstairs so you'll stop worrying. I'm tired and I want to go to bed."

Together they searched all eight bedrooms and attached bathrooms, plus an additional bathroom accessible from the hall.

"This place is a lot bigger than it looks from the front." Colton shoved his gun in his waistband as he met up with Silver outside the stand-alone bathroom.

"Yeah, I wanted the straight, two-story farmhouse look on the front, so it's not very wide. The two short wings on each side form a U in back, which is perfect for the courtyard and outdoor eating area that I set up."

"Your design?"

She nodded absently and rubbed the back of her neck, and he suddenly realized just how exhausted she looked. The emotions of the day had taken their toll.

"Which room is yours?" he asked.

"Room number nine."

"Nine? I only saw eight bedrooms."

"That's because you didn't look in the attic. Come on. I'll show you." She led the way to the end of the hall, where a reading chair and small table and lamp sat in an alcove. Behind them was a decorative fireplace and a chunky oak mantel. She reached underneath the right end of the mantel and a wall panel slid open behind the chair, revealing a dark opening. "Cool, huh?"

He leaned in, his hand resting on his gun, ready to pull it out if necessary. A steep flight of stairs ran along the wall up to the left. A dim light at the top revealed a closed door. "Who all knows about this?"

She shrugged. "Anyone who helped with construction, which is a lot of people around here. They pretty much all pitched in. It was a town project, really, even though I had professional crews. It's not supposed to be a secret or anything. I didn't want the stairs to mar the look of the upstairs hallways and thought this would be fun. It's a cool room, with a large dormer window that overlooks a gorgeous century-old oak tree in the backyard. I'm told it's a good climbing tree, lots of handholds and branches."

"Where's the light switch up there?"

"On the right as you open the door, pretty much where you'd expect it to be. Come on, I'll show you since you obviously want to search my room, too."

"No. Wait here." He ignored her exasperated look as he headed up the stairs. At the top, he pulled out his gun, eased the door open and felt for the light switch. He flipped it on and rushed inside, sweeping his gun back and forth as he made a quick circuit of the rather large room.

The wide window off the back drew him forward. During the day, it would let a lot of light in. He imagined that was the reason the window was so large, so Silver could do her art projects up here. And through the window was the huge oak tree she'd mentioned, framed like a picture, which again he supposed was on purpose. Its thick branches reached out toward the attic window like giant hands, dripping with thick vines. What she thought was beautiful, he thought was a little creepy. And her comment about it being a good climbing tree had him worried. But after seeing how far away from the structure it was, he was reassured that even if someone did climb that tree, they'd never be able to use it as a way to get into the attic window. They'd end up falling to the ground below and breaking their neck.

Even though he was satisfied that no one

could break into her room through that window, he still checked the locks to make sure it was secure.

The creak of a board behind him had him whirling around.

Silver stood in the door opening, her eyes wide as she held her hands out. "It's just me."

He swore and put his gun away. "I told you to wait."

"I don't take orders very well. And you're totally overreacting. The place is empty."

"And locked up tight now. Keep it that way."

She rolled her eyes and plopped down on the king-size bed that dominated the room. "Good night, Colton."

He smiled. "I guess that means you're kicking me out."

"Yes. I am. Your room is—"

"Right below this one. I know. If you need me, just—"

"Tap on the floor?"

"Yeah. That'll work." He crouched down in

front of her and gently swept her bangs out of her eyes. "I'm really sorry for your loss. I know that Eddie meant a lot to you."

She winced when he said Eddie's name, and her eyes took on a haunted look. "Thank you."

He debated giving her the note that Eddie had left her, then decided against it. She was too tired, too…fragile looking. Her insistence on helping him search the house had given her an excuse to push back the pain, to focus on something else if only for a few minutes. And probably her way of feeling that she had some kind of control over her life again. He just hoped she could manage to get some sleep without dwelling all night on the tragedy that had happened.

"Try to get some sleep," he said, giving her hand a squeeze.

"If you ever leave, I will," she grumbled.

He laughed. "I guess I've overstayed my welcome. Good night, then."

"Night."

He rose and headed to the door.

"Colton?"

He paused in the opening and looked back in question.

"I know what…what you did for me, with Garcia. When you were bringing your car around to take me home, your boss told me that you stood up to him, that you took up for me. I just wanted you to know that I appreciate it. After all the lies that I told you, I wouldn't have expected that. So, well, thanks."

He must be going insane, because all he wanted to do was cross the room and pull her into his arms. He was a sucker for a woman in trouble, and that little catch in her voice, the little wobble of her chin as she'd thanked him told him how close she was to losing her composure again. How could he go from being furious with her to wanting to hold her in the span of one day? It made no sense. As soon as they notified Eddie's friends or foster family or whoever needed to be told about his death tomorrow, he was going to get in touch with Drew and tell him to assign someone else to watch over Silver. Because if he hung around her much longer, he wasn't sure that he *could* leave.

"You're welcome," he said, and hurriedly made his escape while he still could.

As soon as the door closed behind Colton, Silver rolled onto her side and buried her face against the sheets. The dam she'd been holding back finally burst and her entire body was racked with sobs. She cried for the pain and fear that Eddie must have endured in his final moments. She cried for a life lost far too soon, for a young man who had never really lived.

By the time she ran out of tears, the moon was hanging low in the sky out her bedroom window and she fell into an exhausted sleep.

BAM!

Silver jerked upright in her bed and clawed for her gun, still holstered to her ankle. She yanked the gun out, sweeping it in an arc around the bedroom. But no one was there.

Bam! Bam!

What was that? She slowly lowered her gun. The sound was coming from downstairs. Along with…voices…and…laughter? She drew in a sharp breath and looked out the window. The sun was fully up. And she suddenly realized what had woken her. The sound of doors slamming.

Oh, no. Her guests were here. Grand opening day. It hadn't even occurred to her last night to cancel the guests' reservations. What was she going to do? She couldn't deal with this right now. But someone had to go downstairs and greet them, tell them the inn was closed.

She ran into the adjacent bathroom to take care of her near-to-bursting bladder and quickly brush her teeth. More noises sounded below-stairs as she thrust her legs into a pair of jeans and threw on a fresh top. A quick run of the brush through her hair and she was groaning at her reflection in the bathroom mirror. Her makeup from yesterday was a smeared mess, but she didn't have time to do much more than rub some of it off with a tissue before running out of her room.

The guests had to be fuming by now that no one was there to greet them. Tippy and Jenks weren't due to arrive until around noon. She'd planned it that way so she could greet all the guests herself and soak in the fun of being her own proprietor. But now everything was a total disaster.

She burst out of the attic doorway onto the second floor.

"Whoa, whoa, whoa."

She saw Colton a split second before she barreled into him. He grunted from the impact but wrapped his arms around her, saving her from a nasty fall. He steadied her with his hands on her shoulders.

"You okay?"

"Yes, fine. Sorry. Let me go. I have to—"

"Hold it. Wait a minute."

She frowned up at him. "The guests are here. I have to—"

"I know the guests are here. But no, you don't have to run down there like the inn is on fire. It isn't. Everything is under control." His gaze dropped down and he cleared his throat before meeting her gaze again. "And as lovely, and I do mean lovely, as you look without a bra, it might not present the professional image you're going for."

She looked down and then drew in a sharp breath and crossed her arms over her chest. The shirt she'd thrown on was white and left nothing to the imagination. "Oh, no," she groaned.

"Don't worry."

The laughter in his voice had her flushing hot.

"Like I said, everything is fine. Tippy and Jenks are here and they've corralled everyone into the dining room and are busily serving an excellent breakfast, or so I've heard. I was just coming up to check on you and see if you wanted some."

She blinked and glanced toward the stairs. "Tippy's here? And Jenks? But I don't understand. They weren't supposed to be here until—"

"Noon. I know. When I checked on you early this morning, you were zonked. Knowing your guests would be arriving soon, I went up to Callahan's Watering Hole—which seems to be the neighborhood hangout around here—and sure enough, it was open. I asked if anyone there knew Tippy, and like you said, everyone knows everyone around here."

"Wait, you're saying the grand opening is a—"

"Success. Yes." His smile faded and he gently brushed her hair out of her face. "Tippy and Jenks know about Eddie, and they were more than happy to come early and take care of things. Freddie said she'd send J.J. over in another hour, just as soon as she finished with the morning rush at Callahan's. You don't have to worry about the inn. Not today."

She searched his gaze, amazed at everything he'd just said. "You did all that, for me?"

He suddenly looked uncomfortable and cleared his throat. "I did all that for both of us. We have to notify Eddie's foster family. I told Tippy and Jenks not to say anything to anyone about what happened until we take care of that. And we can't do that while you're worrying about the inn."

She backed away from him, still holding her arms across her chest. The tears she'd thought she was out of last night pricked the backs of her eyes again. She swallowed hard and held them back. "Well, thank you. I mean, of course you're right. We need to notify his foster parents and foster brothers. Wait, what time is it?"

He pulled his phone out of the holder on his belt. "About nine-thirty. Why?"

"And it's the first of the month, isn't it?"

"Yes. Why?"

"We're too late."

"For?"

"Eddie's foster parents."

He leaned back against the wall. "You've lost me."

"Tony Jones, Eddie's foster dad, works in Naples. He would have left around seven. The kids are all at school. And the mom, Elisa, always goes into Naples on the first of the month, bright and early, to spend their foster program stipend. She won't be back until the kids come home from school."

"Do you have any contact information for them? Or know where the father works?"

She shook her head. "Unfortunately, no."

"Well, waiting is less than ideal. But I don't see where we have a choice." He pushed off the wall and straightened. "Maybe this is a good thing. You can greet your guests and get your mind off everything else for a few hours."

"No. I'm going to take a quick shower. And then we're getting out of here. I can't deal with happy people on vacation right now. And we have something far more important to do while we wait for the Joneses to get home."

"Oh? And what would that be?"

"We're going to find Eddie's killer."

Chapter Eight

Colton paced the upstairs hall for what seemed like forever before he finally heard Silver coming down the attic stairs. As soon as she emerged from the hidden panel, he grabbed her arm and spun her around to face him.

"You don't just say something like that and take off. We need to talk about this."

She shook off his hand and smoothed the dark blue blouse she was now wearing over her jeans. "What is there to talk about? We both know the odds are that whoever killed Eddie is in this town, one of the thugs behind the robberies and the drugs. And I'm going to find out who that is.

I'm through being subtle, taking my time. Because you know what? People get killed while you're dotting all the *i*'s and crossing all the *t*'s. The waiting, the slow, methodical investigating so I can make sure that any evidence I gather will hold up in court, is over. I'm going to figure out who's behind everything. And I'm starting right now."

She headed toward the stairs. He swore and caught up to her, but this time he didn't try to stop her.

"So, what's your plan?" he demanded as they both headed down the stairs.

"My plan is to shake things up and make people nervous. I'm going to flush out the bad guys."

The sound of laughter and the clink of dishes came from the doorway off the foyer that led into the kitchen and dining room. But Silver didn't even pause to look in on her first-ever guests at the inn, or even to talk to Tippy and

Jenks. She flung open one of the front glass doors and marched outside.

Colton shook his head and hurried to catch up to her. She crossed the yard and headed up the street as if she were trying to win a race.

"Where's the fire?" Colton demanded. "Slow down. At least tell me what you mean by 'shake things up.'"

She stopped and faced him, right beside the beginning of the boardwalk at the business next to the B and B. "Look. I appreciate everything you've done for me. I really do. But you're not going to talk me out of this."

"Who said anything about talking you out of it?"

Her look of surprise had him gritting his teeth.

"You're not going to try to stop me?" she asked.

"Last I checked, you're a grown woman with a mind of your own. It's not my place to stop you. But I'd be a terrible friend, and an even worse police officer, if I didn't at least try to discuss this with you so you don't get hurt. You're too close to this. Your emotions could cloud your judgment. You know that. Let me help you. Let's figure this out together."

She blinked up at him. "Friend?"

"What?"

"You said 'friend.' You consider me a friend?" Her unique silver-gray eyes stared up at him in wonder.

"You don't want to be friends?" he asked, completely baffled by her change in subjects. Talking to her was like riding on a runaway train with a switch-happy conductor. He never knew which track the train would take next or whether the train was going to jump the tracks completely.

She slid her arms around his waist, hugging him close. He promptly forgot how to breathe. Good grief, she felt good, her soft curves pressed against him. The tantalizing scent of her shampoo or maybe perfume—he didn't know which—filled his senses. Lust slammed into him so hard and unexpectedly that he had to clench his hands into fists against the urge to slide his fingers through that sexy, short bob of reddish-brown hair and slam his mouth down on hers. Which was crazy. They barely knew each other. How could he want her so much?

"Silver." His voice came out in a hoarse rasp. He cleared his throat. "Silver," he tried again, relieved that he was able to speak coherently. "What are you doing?"

"Hugging you."

He awkwardly patted her back. "I, uh, see that. *Why* are you hugging me?"

"Because we're friends, of course."

"You hug all your friends?"

She sighed and let go of him. "No, Colton. At least, not all the time. I just really needed a hug and you surprised me. Please forgive me. It won't happen again." She whirled around and stepped up onto the boardwalk.

"Oh no, you don't," he growled. He swung her off the boardwalk back down in front of him and pulled her against him, circling her with his arms and resting his cheek on the top of her head. When she just stood there, stiff, unyielding, he said, "In case you can't tell, I'm trying to hug you. I think it's customary for the huggee to put their arms around the hugger. Tit for tat. Or something."

She laughed and hugged him back, resting her cheek against his chest.

Holding her felt so good that he decided not to worry that strangers across the street at one of the businesses were whispering behind their hands. It had been a long time since he'd held a woman, just for friends' sake. Then again, maybe he never had. And even though he still wanted her, just holding her, offering her his support without expecting anything in return, was an entirely new kind of closeness. And he liked it. Maybe she was onto something with this hugging thing.

All too soon, she pushed back and he had to release her.

"Thank you, Colton. I really needed that. And now I feel that I can tackle anything. You're a good hugger, by the way."

He was about to reply when she took off again, hurrying up the boardwalk, forcing him to jog to catch up to her.

"Where are you going?"

"To the heart of Mystic Glades." She pushed through the swinging saloon doors at Callahan's Watering Hole and went inside.

SILVER SCANNED THE dimly lit interior, marking each person that she wanted to interview—and Cato Green was at the very top of her list. She made a beeline toward the bar, which was empty, since the patrons were having breakfast at the round tables. And that suited her just fine.

She climbed onto one of the tall stools that faced the kitchen doorway, barely registering that Colton sat beside her as she waited.

"You're not going to do anything foolish, are you?" Colton asked, keeping his voice low.

"I guess that all depends on your definition of foolish."

"Anything that could make you a target if word gets around to the big fish we're after."

"Big fish, huh? I guess that fits. Whoever's behind Eddie's death is definitely slimy. But to catch a fish, you need bait. And I'm about to bait the hook."

"Maybe we should go somewhere and talk this out first."

"Too late."

The door swung open. Silver reached into her front jeans' pocket.

Cato stopped right in front of her, balancing a tray of breakfast dishes. He looked from her to Colton and back again.

Silver slapped her DEA badge on top of the bar. "Good morning, Mr. Green. When you're finished with those dishes, I'd like a moment of your time."

Cato stared at the badge, and his Adam's apple bobbed in his throat. "I ain't done nothin'."

"I'm sure your parole officer will be happy to hear that. I'll just wait right here while you deliver that yummy-looking breakfast to Freddie's customers."

Cato eyed Colton as though he was sizing him up, then gave Silver a crisp nod and rounded the end of the bar, carrying the tray to one of the tables.

"Mr. Green?" Colton whispered harshly. "Parole officer? The other day you said you thought his name was Cato. But you knew his name, his full name, all along. Are there any other secrets you haven't told me?"

"Probably."

A muscle developed a tic in the side of his jaw. "I wonder what the penalty for impersonating a federal officer is these days. I should have searched your room and taken that badge when I brought you to the inn last night. You do remember that Garcia fired you, right?"

She shrugged. "I remember you telling me he

fired me. But since he didn't tell me himself, how am I to know if you can be trusted?"

He swore.

"You can be mad at me later," she said. "Right now I need your help. Get ready."

"Ready for what?"

"To duck." She gestured toward the mirror above the bar.

Colton followed the direction of her hand. "Ah, hell."

"Duck!"

They both dove to the floor as Cato slammed a chair across the top of the bar, obliterating the chair and sending sawdust and chunks of wood flying around the room. He let out a war cry and whirled around just as Colton leaped to his feet and slammed his fist against the side of Cato's jaw, spinning the larger man around.

Silver scrambled out of the way and grabbed her gun from her ankle holster. "Hands up, Cato," she yelled, aiming her gun off to the side so she wouldn't hit Colton if she had to shoot. Behind her she heard scrambling feet and shouts as the customers hurriedly moved out of the way of the two circling men.

"Cato Green, hands up," she repeated.

Cato let out another yell and charged Colton. Colton slammed his fist into the other man's jaw again. Cato grunted with pain but didn't stop. He barreled forward, wrapping his huge arms around Colton and slammed into a table and chairs.

They fell in a tangle of arms and legs, fists flying, biceps bulging as they each grappled for control.

Silver winced as one of Cato's fists drove into Colton's belly. She glanced around for someone to help, their wide-eyed audience consisting of mostly senior citizens, including Freddie, who was glaring at her from her spot by the far wall.

"You started this, Silver. You're going to pay for everything they break!"

"Sorry," she called out as she shoved her gun into her waistband. She frantically looked around for something to use to help Colton. There, one of the legs of the chair that Cato had busted. She ran across the room and swiped it off the floor.

A loud whack and the sound of shattering glass pinging onto the wooden floor had her whirling around with her makeshift weapon raised. Cato lay unconscious, the remnants of a broken beer mug scattered all around him, except for the handle, which was in Colton's hand as he glared up at her from his crouch on the floor. He tossed the handle into the puddle of soda from whoever's drink he'd grabbed and wiped his hands on his jeans as he stood.

Silver dropped the chair leg and ran to him. "Are you okay? Did he break anything?" She didn't see any blood on him anywhere, but his left cheek was beginning to swell. "We need to put some ice on your face." She reached up, but he glared at her and shoved her hand away.

Without a word, he headed toward the swinging doors.

"Colton, wait." She hurried after him. "Where are you going?"

He waved toward Cato lying on the floor. "This is your mess. You clean it up." And then his brilliant blue eyes met hers, looking darker, angrier than she'd ever seen them. "You can take care of notifying Eddie's foster parents on your own. I'm done."

"Wait, what do you mean you're done? I can fix this. I can—"

Whump. The saloon doors swung in her face. Colton's boots rang on the boardwalk outside as he strode back toward the inn.

Silver's shoulders slumped and she shot an annoyed look at Cato, who was groaning and holding his head as he struggled to sit up.

"Somebody get him a towel," Freddie called out. "And some ice for the lump on his head that I'm sure he's got." When no one moved, she clapped her hands. "Go. Move."

Two of the men hurried over to Cato and crouched down to talk to him while another from their group rushed into the kitchen, presumably to get a towel.

Freddie stopped in front of Silver with her hands on her hips and her flaming red hair looking as if it might actually catch on fire from the red-hot flush on her angry face. "Silver Westbrook, if Jake Young wasn't out of town right now I'd have him arrest you for startin' a bar fight. And it's not even noon. Most people need to get drunk first to do the kind of damage you've done."

"Jake couldn't arrest me, Freddie. He's not a cop anymore."

She leaned down close. "Neither are you, but I saw the flash of the badge you slammed on the bar all the way from my seat over there."

"You knew?"

"Sugar, everyone around here knows you're DEA and that you got fired last night."

She blinked and looked around. Every single person there nodded to let her know they knew.

"Oh, my gosh. All this time, I thought I kept it a secret. How? How did you know?"

"Oh, don't get your panties in a wad. It's just us old-timers that figured it out. We keep up with all our chicks when they leave the nest, knew you'd gone to college to be some kind of lawman. But when you came back to start an inn, well, we might have made a few calls. Your folks mentioned you was working under-cover in the Keys just a few months before you showed up here. We figured you were taking a vacation, but after seeing you snooping around so much we figured you was workin' a case."

Silver put a hand to her head, feeling dizzy from all the revelations. Cato let out a loud curse when one of the women pressed a plastic Baggie full of ice water against his head. He glared at Silver and staggered to a chair they offered him.

"My folks left Mystic Glades years ago," she said. "I didn't think they even kept in touch with anyone back here."

"You figured wrong."

"They wouldn't have known about last night."

"No. But we have friends in the department. Word gets around."

"Wow. It gets around fast."

Freddie hooked a chair with her leg and scooted it over. "Sit down, Silver. We're gonna talk this through and figure it out together." She waved at her circle of friends. "Come on. Pull up a chair. Silver's been on her own long enough worrying about whatever case she's working on. We're gonna help her put the pieces together."

Silver's mouth dropped open as the people she'd always taken for granted as being too oblivious to pay her any attention all pulled up chairs around her like cowboys circling the wagons, only they were circling them for her.

"I don't... I don't know that this is a good idea," she said. "The case I'm working on is dangerous."

"Aren't they all?" Freddie waved her hand again. "This ain't our first rodeo, dear. We helped Jake and Faye sort out their troubles. And Buddy and me helped Amber and Dex solve a murder."

"I didn't think you helped with that," one of the men closest to Freddie said. "I heard Dex did that pretty much on his own."

Freddie narrowed her eyes. "I don't recall asking for your opinion, Dwight."

He swallowed hard and balanced both his gnarled hands on the top of his cane.

"Now," Freddie said. "Where were we? I think, Silver, that you were about to tell us about the case you've been working on. And then you're going to explain what that tall, sexy Colton Graham meant when he said you could notify Eddie's foster parents on your own."

Silver waved toward Cato, who was slowly hobbling toward the kitchen with the help of the two men Freddie had assigned to help him.

"Don't worry about him," Freddie said. "He's not part of whatever you're looking into. He's harmless."

"Harmless? He's an ex-con. I looked into him when I first arrived. He's done time for armed robbery. He's my most promising suspect."

"Sometimes innocent people go to jail. We think Cato didn't get good enough lawyering. He was in the wrong place at the wrong time. That's the only reason he went to jail."

Cato grumbled his agreement as he headed through the kitchen doorway.

"He tried to kill Colton and me because I showed him my DEA badge."

Freddie clucked her tongue and shook her head. "This young generation. You jump to all sorts of conclusions without thinking things through or knowing all the facts. No, Cato wasn't trying to kill anyone. He probably figured he could rough you two up so he could hightail it out the back. You got him riled up on account of mentioning his parole officer. He doesn't want to go back to jail."

Silver slumped in the chair. "If Cato isn't involved, then who is?"

Freddie leaned toward her. "That's what we're gonna help you figure out. But first, what's this about notifying Eddie's foster parents?"

Chapter Nine

Colton held his phone and leaned back against the side of his car on the shoulder of I-75 near mile marker fifty-two. A semi blasted past, blowing hot air in his face and swirling some of his hair in his eyes. He shoved it back impatiently.

"When I get back to Naples, the first thing I'm going to do is get a dang haircut."

"What's stopping you?" Drew said over the phone. "You said Miss Westbrook doesn't want your help."

"That might not be the most accurate slant to what happened," he admitted. "Pretty much she's just not a team player. Instead of letting Homicide investigate Eddie's murder, she decided to amp up the drug investigation, figuring if she found the top guy she'd find the killer. But she went about it all wrong and I, well..." He waggled his jaw where Cato had thrown a particularly hard punch. "I guess I lost my patience with her and told her I was done."

"Huh. That doesn't sound like you."

No, it didn't. He was known for his patience, which was one of the reasons he was so often chosen for undercover work, which tended to move at a snail's pace when he was trying to get in with a bad group of people. It took a lot of time to convince them he was just as bad as them and could be trusted, inasmuch as that type of crowd trusted anyone, even each other. So why was it that he got so frustrated and impatient around Silver?

"Regardless," Colton said, "I just checked out the area around where they found Eddie's body. I was hoping to see some tire tracks or something the forensics guys missed, but there's nothing here."

"Maybe not nothing, exactly," Drew said. "The homicide guys sent me an update on their investigation a little while ago. Hang on a sec." The sound of papers rustling was followed by a thumping noise. "Okay, got it. Yada, yada, yada, yeah, here, second page in. Officers interviewed some morning commuters at one of the rest stops on Alligator Alley and it looks like two different people remembered seeing a car parked on the side of the road in the general area where Eddie was killed, during the time frame we're concerned about. While they didn't see anyone in the car or on the side of the road, they remembered the car itself because of the bright sky blue color and because it was belching out black smoke from the exhaust pipe."

"Sounds like an old diesel maybe?"

"You guessed it. From their descriptions, looks like a Mercedes from the early eighties. Basically an antique. The witnesses said it appeared to be in pristine condition, except for the smoke, of course."

"So our killer likes old cars, and keeps them up. Good to know. And that kind of car would really stand out if I see it somewhere. Anything else in that report?" He idly watched the cars go by as he listened to Drew give him the details, most of which sounded useless for finding the killer, at least now. Sometimes it took one solid piece of evidence to make all the other evidence make sense. "What about Eddie's foster parents? Silver seems to think they're in it for the money, which seems crazy, since there's not a ton of money in taking care of foster kids. Not exactly a get-rich-quick scheme."

"You got that right. I've got friends who foster kids and they spend way more than the state allots them. It's a labor of love for sure, at least with the people I know who do it. Let's see here. The guys are still looking into the Joneses. Found out the father works at a chemical plant here in town, but he's in Alabama at some conference. They did confirm that he bought a car recently."

"You sure he's at the conference?"

"The guys are contacting police in Alabama to do a wellness check. We should know in a few hours if he's really there. You're thinking he killed his own foster kid?"

Colton drummed his fingers against the quarter panel on his Mustang before opening the door and getting in. He started the engine and pulled out onto the highway heading west. He'd have to take the next exit to turn back east toward home. "Just fishing. I have no idea if he's that kind of guy or not. I'm assuming he doesn't have a criminal record, since you didn't mention one. How new is the car he bought? How expensive?"

"Bingo on no criminal record. The wife's clean, too. And the car is about five years old, a Ford Taurus."

The disappointment in his boss's voice mirrored Colton's. Drug dealers or robbery ring runners didn't buy five-year-old cars.

"Doesn't sound like the Joneses are rolling in money," Colton said.

"No. It doesn't. That, unfortunately, is all I have."

"There's an ex-con working in Mystic Glades. He's the cook and maybe bartender, too. Not sure about that. His name's Cato Green. Can you do a quick search on him, see what comes up?"

"Cato Green. Doesn't ring any bells." The tapping sound of Drew's fingers across his computer keyboard echoed through the phone. "Huh, yeah, okay. Looks like he did a few years for robbery. He was the getaway car driver. Claimed he didn't know the guy he was with was robbing the store. Swore he was innocent."

"Don't they all?"

"You got that right. Did a few years. He's on parole. Could be involved. I'll get the guys to dig a little deeper. Any other suspects you want me to add to the list?"

Colton rattled off all the names he knew of people in Mystic Glades, which weren't many. "I really haven't had much of a chance to dig in."

"You weren't supposed to be investigating anyway. Just come on back. Use the rest of the day to get that haircut you've been wanting and spend the night in your own bed for a change. Miss Westbrook can handle the notification to Mrs. Jones this evening. But I'll send a patrol unit out tomorrow to ensure that she's been notified, just in case. I'd hate for his name to get out to the press before everyone who knows him has been told."

"Is the press an issue?" Colton asked.

"Not so far. There was a minor mention of a body found on the highway, but since it's not in the heart of town, there's no big uproar or anything. Still, better to be safe. Mrs. Jones deserves that after taking care of him for however long she did."

"Agreed." He exited the highway and then looped back onto I-75 west this time, toward Naples. Soon he'd pass the hidden turnoff to Mystic Glades, but on the opposite side of the road. The only way to get there from here would be to go to another exit a lot farther down the road and turn around. Or he could just take one of the turnabouts in the median reserved for law enforcement and emergency vehicles. But he wouldn't, of course. There was no reason to return to Mystic Glades.

"Colton? You coming to Naples?"

About a quarter of a mile ahead was a turnabout. He slowed the car, then swore. No, there wasn't any point in going back. Silver didn't want his help. He checked his mirrors, clutched the wheel until his knuckles ached.

"Colton? Hey, man. Should I wait around for you or not?"

The turnabout was coming up fast. Colton

hit the brakes, then jerked the wheel, making the turn.

"Apparently not," he said. "Looks like I've got sucker written all over my forehead."

Drew laughed. "I think it's something else entirely, but I won't go there. She sure is pretty, though."

"That's got absolutely nothing to do with it. I'm just worried…about the case."

"Yeah, keep telling yourself that. Talk to you later."

The call clicked off. Colton tossed the phone into the console.

It was just past noon when he made his way underneath the archway with its alligator-shaped sign. He was a fool for coming back. Silver might need him, but she'd never admit it. She wasn't a team player. And her kind of play was more likely to get him, or herself, hurt or killed than solve a crime.

So why had he come back? He told himself it was out of respect for Eddie's foster mom, that it was his duty to make sure she was told about Eddie's murder. But he very much feared the real reason was a sexy little redhead who was slowly but surely giving him an ulcer.

After he'd parked in front of the inn and checked in with Tippy and Jenks, they told him that Silver had come back almost an hour earlier to get her sketch pad and pencils. But she hadn't told them where she was going. Just to be sure that she hadn't come back and they were busy with guests and didn't notice, he went up to her attic room. But it was empty, and his quick search of the main floor confirmed that she hadn't secluded herself in the office or sunroom either, let alone any of the public areas of the inn. He waved goodbye to Tippy and headed uptown.

He checked out every inch of Main Street. He ducked inside Swamp Buggy Outfitters, which was basically a camping and hunting supply store with an enormous swamp buggy sitting in the front window. But after walking up and down the aisles to make sure Silver wasn't there, he tried Locked and Loaded—a gun store, then Bubba's Take or Trade, and a taxidermy shop called Stuffed to the Gills. He even looked inside Last Chance Church, but he couldn't find Silver anywhere, or anyone who'd seen her since the debacle with Cato earlier.

He'd just passed Callahan's again on his way back to the B and B to search it one more time when a group of about twelve gray-haired citizens descended on him like a horde of slowly moving locusts. The woman in front of the group waved her cane at him and yelled at him to wait for them, so he did, leaning against one of the posts on the boardwalk in front of the saloon while their canes and walkers clicked and clacked on the wooden slats of whatever store they'd come out of.

Good grief. What in the world is this all about?

"See, I told you he'd come back," one of the men in front said as they circled him like a pack of geriatric wolves. "He's sweet on her. He likes Silver."

Colton blinked in surprise. "What? Hey, I'm not *sweet* on her, whatever that means."

"Then why did you come back?"

"It's my job."

"Hey, Freddie," the elderly man called toward the back of their little gathering. "Didn't your friend at the station say that Colton was voluntold to go on vacation for a few days?"

"Yep, he sure did," she called back.

"Then he's not technically working right now. So if he came back to help Silver, it sure looks to me like he's sweet on her."

"Oh, for the love of…stop it. Just stop it." Colton gave them all a look that should have had them running to get out of his way. Instead, if anything, they crowded closer, as if to ensure that he knew they weren't intimidated.

He was really losing his touch.

He held his hands up in surrender. "Okay.

How about I admit that I like her? A little. Will that make you tell me where she is?"

Freddie pushed to the front of the senior squad and crossed her arms over her ample bosom. "Define...a little."

He threw his hands in the air in frustration. "I don't know. I...like I said, I like her. She's interesting. And funny. And smart. And she's kind of adorable when she spaces out and goes off somewhere in her artistic little world that the rest of us don't understand. But she's also frustrating and stubborn and in trouble if she's out there on her own somewhere working on the case. So, please. If you care about her at all, *please* tell me where she is so I can protect her."

Freddie glanced around at her mini-mob. "Well? What do you think? Should we tell him?"

Labron squeezed in between two of the others and took up a stance beside Freddie. "He didn't even mention how pretty she is. I reckon that says a whole lot about how much he likes her, 'cause he likes her for who she is, not for her looks. I'm officially giving my stamp of approval to their relationship."

Colton blinked. Twice. This conversation had gotten so bizarre he didn't even know what to say.

"All in favor of telling him where Silver is?" Freddie asked.

"Aye."

"Aye."

"Tell him."

Cheers went up from all around and Freddie held up her hand so Labron could give her a high five. He grinned and tried, but he couldn't reach it. Freddie laughed and lowered her hand and they slapped palms.

Colton counted silently to five, trying to keep a rein on his temper. "Would someone please tell me where I can find Silver, before she gets hurt?"

"Oh, she's plenty safe. I can see her from here." Freddie pointed across the street to the second story over the shop called the Moon and Star. "With Faye and Jake out of town, she decided to use their apartment upstairs to noodle over everything we told her. She's sittin' in the living room right now trying to figure out who dunnit."

Colton fisted his hands at his sides. Good grief. To think that if he'd just turned around and looked, he'd have seen her silhouetted in the upstairs window by the desk lamp where she was sitting, apparently deep in thought, because she didn't seem to notice her admirers and champions gathered on the street below.

Freddie waved her hand and the senior squad parted like Moses parting the Red Sea, leaving him a clear path across the street.

"Thank you," he managed to say in a civil voice, somehow not shouting even though he wanted to.

"Anytime," Freddie called after him as he strode across the dirt-and-gravel road and then jogged up the steps to the boardwalk in front of the Moon and Star.

The store was dark and a sign in the glass door said Closed. He was about to knock when he decided to just try the knob to see what would happen. Sure enough, it turned easily in his hand.

"Doesn't anyone lock their doors around here?" he grumbled beneath his breath as he stepped inside.

After shutting the door behind him, he threw the dead bolt, relieved that at least the door had a lock on it. He'd half expected that it wouldn't. Now he could be relieved that he didn't have to worry about Freddie's little warriors coming in uninvited to see what was going on.

He wasn't sure what he was going to say to Silver, but for some reason it seemed urgent that he see her. She'd had over an hour and a half since he left to cook up some other crazy scheme. He was already sweating just wondering what fool thing she might want to try next.

He wove his way between tables of what appeared to be exotic potions and perfumes in velvet pouches on various displays. There was jewelry, too, and a few racks of rather interesting clothing that consisted of short, midriff-baring tops and matching skirts that were more silk scarves than anything that would remotely retain anyone's modesty. Just thinking about how Silver might look in a getup like that had his mouth watering and had him cursing himself for a fool. He had to get this attraction to her under control and focus on the danger around them. Because Silver sure as heck wasn't focusing on it and he needed to keep both of them safe.

A quick tour of the bottom floor brought him full circle. Most of the place was the main, open front room that was the shop. There was a small office in the back with a bathroom beside it, and a few other little rooms that looked to be more for inventory and storage than anything else. There was a back door, too, also unlocked.

He shook his head in disbelief and decided to open it and check out back, just to make sure things looked okay. He pushed the door open and something big and black hissed at him from just past the left side of the doorway. He shut the door and bolted it even as his mind struggled to tell him what he already knew.

He'd just been hissed at by a black panther.

Probably the same one that had jumped in front of his car earlier. Great, just one more thing to worry about. He was going to have to warn people that there was a wildcat roaming these woods. Maybe even alert the Florida Panther National Wildlife Refuge southwest of here, back toward Naples. Maybe one of their cats had escaped, or at the least, they might be able to hunt this one down and trap it.

He strode to the opening to the narrow stairs that he'd spotted earlier that led to the second floor. "Ready or not, Silver," he said beneath his breath, "here I come."

Chapter Ten

Stiff from sitting at the desk by the window in
her friend's apartment, Silver closed the blinds
and then worked off her bra from underneath
her shirt. She pitched it onto the desk, kicked
off her shoes and then carried all her drawings
into the center of the living room.

She lay on her belly on the carpet, fanning the
sketches out around her like a dealer in Vegas.
She'd come here hoping the quiet and isolation
would help her get her creative energy flowing
and she'd finally be able to make all the pieces
form the big picture she was searching for. But
as she looked at everything, tapping her pen-

cil against her bottom lip, she couldn't seem to make the pieces fit. There was a key somewhere, something she was missing.

One of the people she'd drawn *had* to be the killer, had to be the man or woman at the top of the criminal food chain who had taken up residence in her hometown. But none of them were leaping out at her as the culprit. And her boss's insistence on slow, methodical approaches meant she had little to show for the months she'd been here—other than setting up her B and B, which she barely even cared about anymore.

She rubbed her tired eyes. What she needed was a break, something that would really take her mind in a new direction. Then she could come back to the notes she'd written on each sketch and make it all make sense.

"Tell me I didn't just get hissed at by a black panther outside."

She jerked up, sitting on the backs of her legs as she clutched her pencil and pressed her hand across her galloping heart. Of all people to be standing in the middle of the living room of her friend's upstairs apartment, Colton Graham was the last person she'd have expected.

His gaze dipped to her chest, reminding her that she'd taken off her bra. Heat flashed through her, and her pulse began to race as she stared up at him. He seemed to drag his gaze up with visible effort and cleared his throat.

"That was probably Sampson," she said. "Faye's pet."

"Someone has a panther as a pet?"

"More or less. He shows up every few days, looking for food. Amy feeds him ground-up meat when Faye's not here to take care of it."

He swore beneath his breath. "I don't care how tame he may seem to your friends. He's still a wild animal, and dangerous."

"He doesn't have any teeth. He can't hurt any-one."

"Does he still have claws?"

"Hmm. Good point." She looked past him to

the door. It was closed, and he'd locked it, had even thrown the chain in place. "I thought you'd left for good. What are you doing here? And how did you find me?"

He looked at the floor, at her drawings. "Freddie told me where you were." He moved around the end of the couch and knelt down beside her, looking at each of her pictures. "You drew Cato? And Buddy? Why? Who are all these other people?" He shuffled through them and picked up the picture of Danny, the boat captain.

He was trying to act as if nothing were happening between them, but the tension was so thick she felt she would die if she didn't touch him soon. Her hand shaking with anticipation, she placed it on his forearm.

His gaze snapped to hers, and a bead of sweat made its way down his temple, even though the air-conditioning was on, keeping the heat and humidity at bay.

"Why are you here?" she asked.

His gaze dropped to her lips, briefly, like a

butterfly's touch, making her pulse leap even more. But then he frowned and looked down at the pictures again. "I was worried…about the case. And I want to help. That is, if you'll listen. If you want my help."

She wanted *him*. And, yes, she wanted his help, too. Needed it. But why couldn't he have been worried about *her*? But then again, she'd given him no cause to see what she'd only come to see herself after he'd stormed out of Callahan's.

She was hooked on him.

She wouldn't call it a crush, although to anyone else it probably would look that way. After all, they'd only met, what, yesterday? But it felt like something so much deeper. And it seemed as if they'd known each other much longer than that. She couldn't get him out of her thoughts, no matter how hard she tried.

"Silver?" His rich, deep voice stroked over her nerve endings, sending delicious shivers straight to the core of her. "Do you want my help?"

She took a chance, and dove into the deep end. "I want *you*." She waited for it to sink in, her face flushing with heat. If he turned her down, she'd feel like a fool, humiliated. But she'd learned long ago, if something was worth having, it was worth fighting for. And that waiting for something to happen might mean it never would. The timing sucked. She should be focusing on the case. They both should. But she also knew how her mind worked, how flustered and unfocused she became the more she tried to concentrate. She needed this. She needed him, to make her world right again. To focus, and to have something, someone, wonderful to hold on to, someone who would be there when all this was over—hopefully. She needed Colton.

He straightened, looking like a nervous stallion scenting a mare, wanting to grab her and flee from her at the same time. His eyes had darkened like a stormy night as his warring needs fought inside him. He didn't bolt. But he made no move toward her, either. Instead, his hands fisted at his sides. A slight hitch in his breathing told her that she had a chance to win this battle.

She rose to her feet, keeping her eyes locked on his the whole time. Slowly, she padded across the thick carpet to stand in front of him, with only a few inches and the heat from both their bodies between them.

"Colton," she whispered. "I want you."

He swallowed, his Adam's apple bobbing in his throat. "We're working on a case. We don't have time—"

"We do have time. Hours to kill before we can go talk to Mrs. Jones." She slid her hands up the front of his chest, delighting in the feel of his muscles bunching beneath the thin fabric of his T-shirt. "And I've got the perfect way to spend at least one of those hours."

"Silver…" His voice came out a harsh rasp. He cleared his throat and tried again, still not touching her, hands at his sides. "I'm not what you're looking for."

"Now, that's where you're wrong, Colton." She slid her hands higher, higher, her fingertips brushing against the heated skin of his neck, tangling with the wild ends of his dark overly long hair where it brushed his collar. He shivered in response, his pupils dilating as he stared down at her like a hungry wolf, ready to devour her. And, oh, how she wanted to be devoured.

She stood on tiptoe, angling her mouth up toward his and pressing herself full against him for the first time. She could feel every thud of his heart where her breasts were flattened against him. "You're exactly what I'm looking for," she whispered. "And you're far too tall. I'm going to need some help here." She tugged the ends of his hair. "Kiss me."

He groaned his surrender deep in his throat a second before he grabbed her and lifted her up, clasping her tightly against him as he captured her mouth in a sweltering kiss. The moment his lips touched hers, everything became right in her world. He kissed away her fears, her

confusion, making everything clear in a spar-
kling, shocking moment of clarity. It was as if
she'd spent her whole life in a fog and he was
melting that away, revealing the world to be far
more beautiful than even her artist's soul had
ever dared to dream.

Rainbows of color burst behind her eyelids as
she soaked in his ravenous hunger, answering
every clever stroke of his tongue with one of
her own, moaning at the exquisite pleasure that
just being held by him in this way sent surging
through her entire body. She was like a match,
bursting into flame as he turned with her and
set her bottom on the back of the couch, freeing
one of his hands to roam over her body.

He broke the kiss, and she whimpered in disappointment. But then he moved to her neck,
lightly sucking her heated skin, nibbling his
way across the sensitive cords and then pulling
her earlobe into his mouth. She arched against
him, gasping with pleasure as her fingers dug
into his shoulders.

Everything in her was melting, softening, readying for him. And she couldn't wait another minute. She fumbled with his belt and quickly unzipped his jeans. He sucked in a sharp breath when she found him, hard and ready for her.

"For the love of…slow down, Silver."

"I don't want to. We can go slow the next time. Please, please tell me you have a condom."

He laughed against the side of her neck. "If not, your friends had better have some around here or I'm going to have to kill somebody. In my wallet, there should be—"

"Don't stop." He'd started to step back to take out his wallet, but she pulled him back to her. "Don't stop."

He framed her face in his hands and captured her mouth again in a kiss that was even hotter, wetter, wilder than the one before. Hello, Dolly, could the man kiss!

She shoved her hands in his back pockets, searching for his wallet, and nearly died of pleasure at the delicious feel of his perfect bottom beneath her searching fingertips. He jerked against her very core, hard, ready. Her fingers frantically plucked at his pocket. A piece of paper crumpled in her hand and she dropped it to the floor. Other pocket, there, his wallet. She hungrily drank in his kiss as she fumbled with his wallet behind his back. As soon as she found the foil packet, she dropped the wallet and pulled back, breaking the kiss.

She shoved his jeans down his hips, then reached for his boxers.

He tipped her chin up, forcing her to look at him. "Silver, I want you, more than anything. But this is so soon. Are you sure that you—"

She pushed his underwear down, freeing him. He swore and jerked against her in all his glory. Her breath left her in an unsteady rush. "Oh, I'm sure. Am I ever! You're beautiful, perfect." She rolled the condom onto him and gave him a powerful, long stroke, worshipping him with her hands.

He whispered sexy words in her ear, telling

her exactly what he wanted to do to her while his fingers made quick work of her jeans and panties, lifting her bottom off the couch while he raked them away. And then he was poised at her entrance, and they stared into each other's eyes.

His hands shook as he slid one hand around her back and adjusted himself with the other. "It's not too late to say no. It will probably kill me to stop, but I will."

"You *see* me, Colton. The real me." She feathered her fingers down the side of his face. "You understand me like no one else ever has. This is what I want. You're what I want." She pressed a soft kiss against his lips and pulled back to look at him again. *"Don't. Stop."*

His entire body shook with need as he clasped her tightly to him and surged forward. Pleasure zinged through her unlike anything she'd ever felt. He was made for her. And she was made for him. Every thrust of his body, every maddeningly clever stroke of his fingers against her most sensitive spot as he made love to her had her arching against him and matching his rhythm with hers.

Every drawing she'd ever done, every painting she'd ever created in her search to show the true beauty of life seemed to culminate in this moment. Instead of painting him on canvas, capturing his likeness with pencil or pen, she drew him inside her, his every stroke like a master artist wringing out the beauty of this moment, creating the most incredible, eloquent masterpiece ever imagined.

And then he lifted her in his arms, turning with her, staggering down the short hallway to the sparse bedroom that was obviously the guest room on the right. Without breaking away from her, he gently laid her down, his strokes slower now, more delicious, his body shaking as he obviously made every effort to hold himself back, to make this last.

Her shirt was suddenly gone over her head,

and his hot breath washed over her as he clasped one of her nipples into his mouth and sucked.

"Colton!" She arched off the bed, drawing her knees up as she came apart in his arms, soaring to planes she'd never known existed as the colors burst behind her eyelids.

He lavished her other breast with the same attention, his strokes coming harder and faster as he rode her through her climax. And then his hands were on her again, rebuilding the delicious tension inside her, impossibly bringing her higher than she'd been before.

As she catapulted into another wave of pleasure, her name burst from his lips and he joined her, clasping her tightly against him as he spent himself in her arms.

EVEN BEFORE COLTON opened his eyes, he knew he'd made a mistake. Well, not a mistake exactly. Making love to Silver had probably been the highlight of his existence and he wouldn't want to undo it, even if he could. There were no words in his vocabulary equal to the task of describing how right it had felt being with her. After this, he couldn't imagine ever being with another woman. Ever.

That was the problem.

What was he supposed to do now? Go down on bended knee and ask a woman he'd just met to marry him? She'd think he was crazy. Hell, he thought he was crazy. And it wasn't as though he wanted to get married. The thought had never even crossed his mind. His career always came first. And while he adored women, he'd never loved one. Never planned on loving one. And since he didn't believe in love at first sight, what, exactly, had happened to him?

All he knew for sure was that he needed distance—from this case, from Silver, from the disaster his life had just become. He needed to think and figure out what he was going to do. Giving up his career, months of being undercover where there was no room or time for a family, wasn't an option. Which meant after this investigation was over, he'd go his way and Silver would go hers. That was the only way this could end. But when he tried to conjure a picture of his future without Silver Westbrook, all he could see was a big, black void.

Man, was he in trouble!

"Wake up, sleepyhead." Silver's warm, soft hand patted his abdomen. "We have work to do, a case to figure out."

That one, simple touch awakened his body again, making his pulse leap through his veins and hardening him almost instantly. He gritted his teeth and willed his body back under control.

"Colton? Are you okay?"

Nope. Not under control. Even her voice had lust crashing through him. What he needed was a stiff drink. Maybe that would take care of his…stiff problem. He groaned at his own pun and forced his eyes open.

The bed dipped and Silver braced her hands on the mattress on either side of him, her face a mirror of concern. "Did you hit your head on the headboard or something?"

Since his body had become invaded by some kind of emotional wreck of a man whom he didn't recognize, he went with it, dragging her down for a kiss, all the while hoping he'd been wrong and that kissing her wasn't nearly as incredible as he remembered.

Nope. It wasn't like what he'd remembered. It was better.

He groaned and ended the soul-shattering kiss that had him hard and aching beneath the comforter. She'd ruined him. And he didn't have a clue what he was going to do about it.

She blinked down at him. "Wow. I don't even want to know how many women you've kissed to become that great at it. The jealousy would kill me. Now get up and get dressed. I'm all focused again now—thank you for that, by the way—and ready to solve this case."

She hopped off him and sashayed into the living room, already dressed and acting as if their lovemaking hadn't knocked her off her axis as it had him. What had she said? She was *focused* again, thank you? He frowned. Did she have sex with near strangers often, to focus her thoughts?

That dark thought had a little green monster poking him in the vicinity of his heart. And he didn't like it one bit. A drink. Yeah. He definitely needed something to take the edge off. And he didn't care that it wasn't five o'clock yet. It was five o'clock somewhere.

He rolled onto his side and looked for his clothes before remembering they were on the living room floor. And he was lying here with a hard, aching erection. Going out there and waving that around was a recipe for disaster. If she even looked at him as though she might want another roll in the hay, he'd probably tackle her to the floor and do all the things he desperately wanted to do to her that he hadn't done yet. No. He couldn't go out there naked. In that way lay danger. He'd just have to wrap the comforter around himself and go get them.

He slid his legs out of bed and held the comforter over his lap, about to get up, when Silver came back in carrying his things.

"Oh, hey." She smiled. "I just remembered you didn't have your clothes with you." She waved at the adjacent bathroom. "Want me to put them in there in case you want to wash up?"

He smiled tightly, or tried to. But he wasn't in a smiling mood and rather doubted he'd succeeded by the way her gorgeous silver-gray eyes widened.

"Sure, thanks," he said.

"O…kay." She set his things on the counter. "Oh, I almost forgot." She stepped back to him. "I accidentally pulled this out of your pocket earlier when I was, well, you know, looking for your wallet." She held her hand out toward him, holding a folded sheet of paper.

The paper that Drew had given him at the station.

He'd completely forgotten about it.

"Colton?" She continued to hold the paper

out. "Is something wrong? If this is private, no worries. I didn't read it."

"It's yours."

"What?"

He grabbed her empty hand and tugged her to the bed. "Sit. Please."

She sat beside him and waited, the paper still in her hand. He set it aside and took both her hands in his, half-turning to face her, with one leg folded beneath him on the bed.

"Remember back at the station, when you left the room after finding out about Eddie?"

She stiffened, a shuttered look entering her eyes. "Yes. Of course I remember."

"That piece of paper is an email the Miccosukee police sent to Drew. It's a copy of a letter. The original was found in an envelope at the crime scene." He picked it up and unfolded it, then held it out toward her. "The envelope was addressed to you. And this is the letter that was inside. I'm sorry it's taken me this long to give it to you. At first, I was worried how you'd take it. And later, it slipped my mind. I know that's not an excuse. I really am sorry."

Her eyes filled with tears and she quickly wiped them away. "You read it. I can't."

"Silver—"

"Please. Just read it out loud." She closed her eyes, her hands fisting against the sheets.

Colton sighed and began to read.

"Dear Miss Westbrook. Can I call you Silver? I always wanted to, but it didn't seem respectful enough. But since this is good-bye, maybe you'll forgive me this one time.

"You were always a really good friend to me, and the only adult who really, truly seemed to care what happened to me, and whether I studied or ditched class. Because you wanted me to make something out of my life.

"I'm sorry to say that I let you down.

"Me and some of the guys got into some things that we shouldn't have. That blue vase?

It was stolen, and some of the other things I brought you. Stupid, I know. It started out as a onetime thing, a dare. But it grew from there. And other stuff happened, stuff I'm too ashamed to talk about in this letter. And once I was in, I couldn't get out. That stupid attempted holdup? Yeah, I could tell you knew it was me. And I was so ashamed because you just wanted to help me, protect me, and I was there to take money, jewelry, anything I could get—I would have taken yours, too. Please know that I had good intentions. To help some friends. I can't say anything else because I don't want them to get into trouble."

"He was talking about the drug ring, wasn't he?" she asked.

"I think so," he said. "That's what Drew thinks, too."

She nodded. "Please, go on."

Colton searched for where he'd left off in the letter, then continued.

"Well, I've found a way out. I'm turning the thefts into something good and helping some people, some friends. But I can't stick around, because what I've done will send me to jail once it's out. And I could never survive a place like that. But at least I'll have done some good by helping others out. You should be proud of me for that."

She squeezed her eyes tightly shut, but tears rolled down her cheeks.

"Want me to stop?" he asked. "We can finish this later."

"No. I want to hear all of it. Go on."

"I'm sorry I left without saying goodbye. I'm starting a new life somewhere else. I don't want to go to jail, so I had to do it this way. I promise I won't get into trouble again.

"Goodbye, Silver.

"Your friend,
"Eddie."

He folded the paper and handed it to her. She took it between both hands and shook her head. "I told you that he was a good kid. He made mistakes, and he wanted out. He tried to fix things. He was a good kid," she repeated.

Colton wasn't so sure he agreed, but it obviously meant a lot to her that he believe her. He put his arm around her shoulders and held her close. "He was a good kid." He kissed the top of her head and rubbed her arm, gently rocking her against him as she absorbed the contents of the letter.

Finally, she sniffed, wiped her face and pushed away from him. "When you first got here, you asked if I needed your help. I do. Very much. Help me find Eddie's killer?"

"Of course."

"Thank you. I'll wait in the living room." She got up and hurried toward the door.

"Silver?"

She paused and turned, looking at him expectantly.

"I'm not going to stop until we find the creep who killed him. You have my word."

Her jaw trembled and her eyes shone over-bright with more unshed tears. She nodded her thanks and pulled the door shut.

Colton groaned and collapsed back onto the bed. He knew better than to promise something he couldn't really control. He knew from experience that no matter how hard he might want to crack a case, sometimes the evidence just wasn't there.

Chapter Eleven

Silver sat down on the carpet in the living room again. But this time she was fully dressed—bra and all—and there was a deep, burning thirst for justice inside her belly that she hadn't felt in a long time. Yes, she'd wanted to catch Eddie's killer before she'd read that letter, or rather before Colton had read it to her. But knowing that Eddie had finally gotten it, that he'd realized he needed to turn his life around, and then that he'd had that life snatched away so brutally, had focused all her emotions into a deep-seated need to do this last thing for her friend—to bring down whoever had taken his future away from him.

And now that she had Colton to help her do it, she finally believed that this case could be solved, that together they would find justice, and Eddie Rafferty could rest in peace—God rest his soul.

Colton came out of the room and sat down beside her. He picked up a couple of the drawings. "Catch me up to speed. What is all this?"

"Suspects," she said, thumping the picture of Cato with her pencil. "Or potential suspects, I suppose. After you left earlier this morning, Freddie and her friends helped me brainstorm who could be the real bad guy. And these are the people we came up with. I added a few of my own, but mostly this is from the group, uh, meeting that we had." She shrugged. "Drawing anything that's bothering me helps clarify things in my head. Normally. No luck today, though. At least, not earlier. I'm hopeful that together we can figure it out."

His jaw tightened, as if he wasn't so sure. But he nodded his agreement. "I see you drew Buddy. Why not Freddie, too?"

"She's harmless."

"But Buddy isn't? They're a lot alike, about the same age, feisty, strong, stubborn. I wouldn't peg either of them as being able to hurt a physically fit eighteen-year-old. But ordering someone else to do it? Yeah. I can totally see that."

"Hmm. I'm not sure that I agree. I certainly can't picture Freddie doing anything like that. She might be a Brillo Pad on the outside, but inside she's a squishy sponge. Buddy's a lot like her, a really nice guy at heart."

He shook his head. "Yeah. I saw that nice heart when he charged you for an airboat ride that he pressured you to take. And when his staff charged crime victims four bucks for bottles of water at the south dock."

"Okay, okay. So he takes making a profit a bit to the extreme." At his incredulous look, she said, "A *lot* to the extreme. Agreed. But that doesn't make him a killer. And if you were down-and-out, he'd be one of the first in line to step up and help."

"If you say so. But if you believe that, why did you draw him?"

She picked up Buddy's picture and pointed to the notes written on the bottom. *"Organizer, leader, tends to be arrogant.* Those characteristics made me include him. He does love money, and he's driven to make as much as he can, even though he doesn't ever spend much. It's the thrill of it. He's competitive. I can totally see him as a guy in charge, organizing, making things happen. But even if he was the guy at the top, I seriously doubt he'd do it if he knew anyone was stealing or there were drugs involved. Someone could be taking advantage of him, stroking his ego, using his resources and knowledge of the area to run the operation without him even realizing what's really going on."

He took the picture from her and read the rest of the notes that she'd written, dates and times when she'd seen him with Eddie and other young teenagers, or in conference with Cato and others. "He does run those airboat tours. Airboats would be a perfect way to get goods into Mystic Glades, up through the canals. But he'd need another way to distribute them from there, onto the streets, without making anyone suspicious." He handed the picture back to her. "There may be something to your theory about someone using him without him knowing it. So who would use the airboats—when they're not running tours? How many boats are there?"

"Three. But if someone takes them out after the tours, they'd be noisy. We'd hear that."

"I remember seeing that captain on our boat—"

"Danny."

He nodded. "During the holdup, he used a pole to push the boat to shore. Looked fairly easy and didn't make any noise. If he or the other boat captains are in on this, they could push the boats away, or even pull them out into a canal using a canoe or kayak before turning that noisy engine on."

"I'd hate to think that Danny or the other boat pilots were involved. He seems so nice."

"How long have you known him?"

"Not long. He's one of the men Buddy hired just this summer. He doesn't live around here."

"We should look into his background, then. And keep him on our suspect list. When I spoke to Drew earlier, I listed Danny, along with everyone else whose name I could remember. He's having the team run background checks on everyone. We'll check back with him tomorrow and see if they've found anything useful."

"Drew, your boss? You spoke to him?"

"When I left Callahan's, I drove out to Alligator Alley and called him. The homicide team found some witnesses who saw a rather unique car near the crime scene at the right time— a nineteen-eighties sky blue Mercedes. It belches black smoke, so I figure it's probably one of the early diesels. Seen anything like that around here?"

"Honestly, it's so rare that I see cars around here. And I'm not much of a car person. I can hardly tell one model from the next."

"What kind of car do *I* drive?" he asked.

"A black Mustang GT."

He smiled. "Seems to me like you *do* pay attention to cars."

She waved her hand. "No, that's just because it's *your* car. Of course I remember what kind you drive."

His eyes widened and her face heated. Just because they'd made love didn't mean that he felt about her the way she'd already accepted that she felt about him. She was getting way too comfortable around him, letting things slip that she'd rather not share. If she wasn't careful, he'd realize how much she craved being around him. Which would be nothing short of humiliating if he didn't share the same affliction.

Even when he was mad at her, she wanted to

see his handsome face, listen to that rich baritone soothe her troubled spirit. That was it really, the reason she was so drawn to him, and why he seemed like the yin to her yang. It was because he *understood* her and made her feel comfortable in her own skin. That was such a rare gift, and she'd never experienced it with anyone else.

And, of course, after that practically out-of-body experience of making love with him, she couldn't exactly discount the physical part of their attraction. It was almost as though her soul recognized a kindred spirit in him, and her body recognized it, as well. Making love with Colton had changed her forever. She just wished she knew whether he felt the same.

"You mentioned you don't see many cars," he said, apparently deciding to let her Mustang comment go. "Why is that?"

"There aren't many cars around here to see. The residents who live in apartments above the businesses on Main Street generally walk to get where they need to go. Others walk if their homes aren't too far back in the woods. Cars are for those who work outside town, so they don't tend to drive down the main street. They go down a side road that heads into the trees. The few who do drive cars into town tend to park them behind the businesses that have parking lots, like Swamp Buggy Outfitters. And still more use canoes, kayaks or ATVs to get around."

She pitched her pencil down. "Maybe there's no point in even looking at these. Maybe Garcia's right and I suck at being an agent. I was going to quit anyway, start a new career as a bed-and-breakfast owner. So I must have known, subconsciously, that there wasn't much point in my continuing as an agent."

He stood and pulled her to her feet and then gently tilted her chin up. "Whatever Garcia said is irrelevant. That man couldn't find his own socks if they were sitting right in front of him. Forget him."

She laughed, some of the tightness easing in her chest. "I think you have him pegged."

He stepped back and bent down, scooping up the pictures. "Let's see if we can't figure this thing out before we go notify Mrs. Jones this evening."

He held the drawings up and motioned toward the table in the eat-in kitchen that was really just an alcove off the main room. "We might be more comfortable in there."

"Good idea. Have you eaten lunch? It's getting closer to the dinner hour than lunch but still too early for me to wait that long. I'm starving. I could check the fridge and see what Jake and Faye have in there. I'm sure I can whip up something decent."

"I could eat. Maybe sandwiches or something light. We can work on them together. And while we do, you can tell me who Jake and Faye are—and why you're in their apartment."

While they worked in assembly-line fashion putting together two rather impressive ham-

and-cheese subs with all the fixings, she told him about the owners of the Moon and Star, Jake and Faye, and how they were out of town on a second honeymoon trip along with friends of theirs, Dex and Amber. Dex was paying for the trip because Jake and Faye had cut their honeymoon short to help him when he was in trouble.

"Sounds like you like Faye and her husband very much. I can hear it in your voice." He set their plates on the table. "Chips? I saw some in the pantry when I got the bread out."

"Sure." She opened the refrigerator. "Want a soda? Or beer?"

"Water. Beer would be my preference, but I want a clear head for the case." He stepped into the walk-in pantry. "You were going to explain why you're in this apartment instead of in your room at the B and B."

"Isn't it obvious? There are a ton of people over there right now. I needed peace and quiet to concentrate." She grabbed two cold water bottles.

"Tell me about it. I was over there earlier looking for you."

He moved her drawings to the counter before setting a bag of chips on the table. The almost reverent way he treated her work, even if it was just quick, throwaway-quality sketches, had her feeling all funny inside. She might not know squat about his past, but everything he'd done from the moment he met her had been designed to protect her and others. And he always treated her with respect, never looking at her as if she were crazy or flighty, the way so many people in her life did. Instead, whenever she spaced out, he found it amusing. So many people had gotten exasperated with her, or had mocked her for what she really couldn't help.

If her boss had seen her sketching suspects, he'd have told her to stop wasting time. But Colton respected her methods even if he didn't understand them. He hadn't even batted an eye at her drawings. And his questions were spoken with genuine curiosity, not disdain.

"Earth to Silver," he teased, waving a hand in front of her face. "Where did you go there?"

She shrugged. "Nowhere important. Let's eat, and try to narrow our list of suspects."

She hadn't realized how hungry she was until she took the first bite of her ham-and-cheese sandwich. Then she practically inhaled it.

"Hungry much?" Colton grinned, with over half his sandwich still left.

Her face heated. "I didn't have breakfast."

"And I did. Totally understandable." He leaned to the side and pulled a knife out of a drawer without having to get up in the tiny kitchen. After cutting off the part of his sandwich that he'd eaten from, he set the rest of it on her plate. "Be my guest."

The half sandwich did look tempting. But she couldn't possibly eat it when the incredible male specimen in front of her had barely eaten anything. She'd be embarrassed.

He tilted her chin up again. "Hey. I can tell you're still hungry. So eat. As tiny as you are, it's not like you have anything to prove."

Her stomach chose that moment to growl.

Colton laughed and shoved her plate closer to her. "Go on. You eat while I ask a few more questions."

"About what?" she said, holding a hand up in front of her mouth, since she'd already taken a bite.

"Charlie Tate and Ron Dukes, the young men you first saw with Eddie the day you found that kilo. I noticed you didn't draw them."

She chased her bite of sandwich with a quick drink from her bottle of water. "That's because they aren't around anymore. Charlie's family had been going to therapy and jumping through hoops with the Department of Children and Families and were finally approved to take him home. So they did, in Naples. And I haven't seen Ron in a couple of weeks."

"Doesn't that strike you as odd?"

"That Charlie moved, no. Ron? Yeah. I wondered if something had happened to him. I followed up as best I could, but he didn't really have any friends in town. And nothing came up in any missing persons databases. No crimes or unsolved homicides that involved anyone fitting his description. My boss told me to keep my focus on our most promising—and remaining—suspect, Eddie. Even before Ron disappeared, I pretty much spent every free moment when I wasn't working on the B and B keeping tabs on Eddie. But I was limited in what I could do because of using the B and B as my cover. There were big gaps in the day when I was stuck at the inn and couldn't say where Eddie was. But as to where Ron is right now, I couldn't tell you."

He sat back in his chair, seemingly lost in thought as he looked past her.

She quickly finished the rest of her sandwich, giving him the time he needed to think things through. But when she started clearing the dishes, he got up and helped her. They worked together in a comfortable silence until everything was put back the way it should be. And then they attacked the guest room, changing the sheets and putting everything to rights. Silver couldn't bear the teasing if her friend somehow figured out that she'd slept there with Colton. Faye would be thrilled for her, of course, but Silver was more private than Faye and preferred to keep things, well, private.

They returned to the living room and straightened up in there, too, before Silver headed back into the kitchen.

"I'll have to remember to take out the garbage when we leave," she said. "Faye and Jake get back in about a week. I wouldn't want them to come back to a smelly kitchen."

He braced his shoulder against the kitchen wall. "What do residents of Mystic Glades do, just set the garbage out back and someone picks it up?"

"No, there's a collection of Dumpsters a quarter mile back in the trees, northeast of the entrance. Everyone hauls their trash there. It's picked up three times a week so it won't smell too bad."

"It's hard to imagine a garbage truck making that tight U-turn on I-75 to go down the road by the culvert to get here, let alone drive the five or six miles past the fence. And three times a week? We don't even get that kind of service back in Naples."

"It's more like eight miles from I-75," she said absently as she leaned back against the counter. "And you're right, the county doesn't send a truck. Our town purchased its own special truck years ago that we keep parked in the woods. The truck is used to unload the Dumpsters and carries everything to a garbage-processing facility several miles out of town, way back in the woods." She stared up at him. "It all goes out on a small barge every week, down the canals to a collection point. The county takes it from there."

He grew still and returned her stare. "A barge. Every week."

She slowly nodded. "Are you thinking what I'm thinking?"

"That our drug dealer doesn't need the air-boats to deliver his drugs? Yeah. That's what I'm thinking. Who owns the barge operation?"

"The same person who runs everything else around here. Buddy Johnson."

"No surprise there. He probably charges everyone here for trash collection, and gets a check from the city, too."

"I think so, yes."

"And who does all the work?"

"High school kids take turns running the truck from the Dumpsters to the facility. It's a quick trip, probably takes no more than an hour to empty the Dumpsters, haul the contents to the site, then park the truck back by the Dumpsters. A different kid does it each time so it doesn't infringe on their homework time. And

Buddy pays them pretty well. It's quick, easy work. The truck takes care of all the lifting."

"I'm guessing Eddie was one of the kids doing that."

She nodded. "Yes. And Charlie, and several others."

"What about the processing of all that garbage into bales and loading it onto the barge once a week? Who oversees that?"

"It used to be Ron Dukes. But after he disappeared, someone else took over."

He braced his arm on the countertop. "Who?"

"Cato Green. It's his weekend job now, to supplement the money he makes at Callahan's during the week. Colton, I think you need to make another call to your boss. We need to find out where Ron Dukes went, and see if Drew has found out anything else about Cato."

He arched an eyebrow. "I think we both know where Dukes probably ended up."

She swallowed against the bile rising in her

throat. "The county dump, after taking an involuntary ride on a barge full of garbage."

"It's a perfect setup. Anyone who crosses the boss, or makes a mistake, can be hauled out with the trash. No one would have any reason to search through a barge full of bundled-up garbage thinking there'd be a dead body. And what do you want to bet that the kilos are in one of those bundles, and they get off-loaded onto another boat right before the barge reaches the collection point? Mystic Glades could be a distribution point for all of south Florida. But if that's the case, why kill Eddie on the side of the highway and leave him there for others to find when they could have just taken him out on the barge? You think the killer was sending a message?"

"I do. Unfortunately, in my job—or former job—investigating drug dealers," she said, "that's not uncommon. Whoever killed Eddie wanted him to be found. It was a message, maybe a warning to others who knew Eddie, others who were working with the same boss, not to cross him. Drug dealers are known for sending messages like that. But where does the burglary ring fit in with all this?"

"It doesn't, not at first blush," he said. "I can't imagine a drug dealer running a ring like that out of the same place as his base of operations, his distribution point. Why risk bringing any scrutiny that could destroy his whole operation? The drugs have to be raking in hundreds of thousands of dollars, if not millions, depending on how many kilos he's funneling through here. Burglary, even from wealthy homes, isn't nearly as profitable. At least, not based on the lists of stolen goods I've been working with. And the logistics, the location of buyers and the risks are completely different."

"Maybe the two aren't related?"

He shook his head. "What would be the odds of two major crime hubs in one tiny town that aren't related? There has to be something else that explains the link. The note that Eddie left

certainly made it sound like the burglary ring
and drug ring were connected. I didn't have
the kind of proof to go to court and build a
case against Eddie yet for the thefts, but I had
enough to know he was deep into it, even before we read his pseudo-confession. That's why
I wanted to use him, to get him to turn against
his boss and make a deal. But I never got the
chance. As for the drug part, you saw him with
a kilo. Even if that was the first, it obviously
wasn't the last." He pulled his keys out of his
pocket. "We can speculate on that later. You
said the barge won't run until the weekend.
What about the Dumpster pickup? When is the
next day that's scheduled?"

"Tomorrow night."

"Good. We can check it all out now while
there's no one around, and look into that barge
operation, see if it really makes sense that it
could work the way we're thinking. If our suspicions seem feasible, then we'll head out to

Alligator Alley, where I can get cell phone coverage and call Drew."

"Right," she said, fisting her hands at her sides. "So he can investigate Cato. And send someone out to the county dump, with cadaver dogs."

Chapter Twelve

Silver wrinkled her nose as Colton drove his Mustang down the narrow dirt road past the Dumpsters and toward the barge operation. "I can see why they have this place so far away from town. No one wants to smell this every day."

"Yeah, I can't imagine Buddy wanting the aroma to interfere with his tourism plans for the town." The trees opened up ahead, revealing patches of blue sky. "Let's assume someone could be here even though we think it's deserted."

"My pistol's loaded." She patted her jeans over

her ankle holster. "And I don't ever intend to leave home without it again."

He pulled the car over into a patch of gravel that appeared to be for parking and cut the engine.

They both got out and surveyed the huge clearing. There wasn't a lot to it. Just a metal building on the right with enormous containers hooked to the outside of it—probably where the teenagers emptied the trucks. And there was a steel conveyor belt coming out of the building leading toward the swamp. It looked a lot like what she'd seen at airports, the metal rollers she pushed her suitcase on, along with the plastic containers that held her shoes, so it could feed the X-ray scanners.

"Looks fairly automated," Colton said as they crunched through the dirt and gravel to where the conveyor ended.

A small barge, a miniature version of what would normally be seen on a river carrying boxcars to a dock, was tied up to a bulkhead.

It appeared to be designed to keep the swamp from encroaching on the land, ensuring deep enough water for a heavily loaded barge to not get stuck.

"There's a small crane on the barge," she pointed out. "I guess they dump the garbage into the large containers, and then the trash feeds into the building to be bundled. All they have to do is run the bundles down the conveyor and use the crane to load it. What do you think? A two-man operation?"

"Easily. One person could do it if he had to. And it wouldn't require anyone with much skill."

"That explains why Cato was hired. He's not the brightest bulb in the box." She put her hands on her hips and scanned the area again. "It looks amazingly clean around here. Far more kept up than I'd expect of a garbage facility."

"I was thinking the same thing. Stay alert. Let's check out the building."

He drew his pistol and she did the same. Better safe than sorry. They kept their weapons pointed down toward the ground as they approached the opening. There was no door. The building was more like a small aircraft hangar, open on one side. The smell was worse inside than out by the containers. But underlying the familiar odor of garbage was…something else. She sniffed, trying to identify the smell. It was familiar, too, and not unpleasant, just…not what she'd expect here.

They performed a quick search of the building, but it was clearly empty except for the baling machine hooked up to chutes on the container side of the facility.

"What *is* that?" she asked, sniffing again. "It seems like it's coming from—"

"Over here." He crouched beside the baling machine and picked up a piece of gravel from the ground. He sniffed it and jerked back, holding it away from his nose. "This is the source, for sure." He pitched the rock down and stood, pointing at the base of the machine. "Someone splashed it all over the ground here, and the bottom of the machine. See how the paint's peeling there?"

When she reached him, she nodded in agreement. "Bleach."

"Yep. And what do criminals use bleach for? Especially this large an amount?"

"To destroy blood evidence."

He kept his back to the walls, his gun at the ready as he scanned the clearing, visible through the opening to the building. "Let's get out of here."

Her mouth went dry as she followed him to the entrance. Living in a remote area like Mystic Glades, being surrounded by woods and trees and hemmed in by acres of saw grass and marsh had always seemed like a mecca, a blessing. It was like living inside an extraordinary painting that one of the masters had left for lesser artists like her to soak in and enjoy. But right now, realizing how far away from town she and Colton were, isolated—and suspecting that someone could have been murdered in the building behind them—had her hands going clammy and her heart racing as if she'd just run a marathon.

He waved her to stop at the opening as he looked outside. It was a long, quiet minute before he motioned her forward, and she followed him around the corner. They hurried to his car and hopped inside. The wheels spit up gravel as he took off toward town. It wasn't until they were back at the archway that announced the entrance to Main Street that she finally relaxed against the seat and holstered her gun. Colton hesitated, idling the car.

Silver pushed her hair out of her face with a hand that was embarrassingly shaky. "What are you doing? Don't you want to head out to the highway to call Drew?"

He nodded and checked his phone. "Yeah, and I will. But between the time we spent at your friend's apartment and the time that it took to look over that garbage facility, it's already past six."

"Mrs. Jones. I completely forgot. And Freddie and her close circle of friends know about Eddie. We really do need to officially notify her before she finds out from someone else."

"I was thinking the same thing. How far away is her house?"

"If you turn left here instead of going down Main Street, and circle around behind that first business, there's a little road that heads east to several different homes. The Joneses' house is pretty much at the end, about five miles or so down."

"All right. Let's get that taken care of. Then we'll circle back to the B and B and get you an overnight bag. I'd like to sit with Drew and the other detectives and talk all this through. If he thinks our theory is worth looking into, he can send that team to the dump, and we'll plan on bringing a CSI team back here in the morning to go over the garbage facility to see if the cleanup missed anything. We can try to get a warrant, but our best bet will probably be just to get Buddy Johnson's permission. If neither of those happens, we'll surround the facility and sit on it until we get something that can convince a judge to issue the warrant. But I don't want to do anything tonight that will alert someone to go out there and scrub that place any more than it's been scrubbed."

"Sounds like a plan. You mentioned an overnight bag. Is there a hotel close to the station where I can stay?"

"Yes. But you're not staying there. You're staying with me, at my apartment." He glanced over at her, his expression unreadable. "You okay with that?"

She expected him to explain his reasons, like that he wanted to keep her nearby so they could discuss the case. But when he didn't say anything, she realized what this was—his way of saying, finally, hopefully, that making love to her hadn't been a onetime thing. That maybe there was a future here. That he was interested in a relationship with her. And she wasn't about to say no to that.

"I think it's a great idea," she said.

He gave her a curt nod. "Good." He shifted gears and sent the Mustang down the road toward the Joneses'.

LEAVING THE COMFORTING of Mrs. Jones to Silver, now that they'd broken the news about Eddie to her, Colton—with Mrs. Jones's permission—walked through their one-story house, looking for clues, anything that Eddie might have left behind that could help them figure out who he'd associated with and which one of them might be the one pulling the strings.

The house was a typical ranch house, but built on four-foot-high stilts to keep it high and dry whenever storms or late-afternoon summer rains caused the swamp to encroach on the property. Colton had noticed that all the houses they'd glimpsed back in the trees when driving here were built on stilts. She'd told him that there were only a few that weren't, like a mansion down a different road that the founder of Mystic Glades had built. It was on a solid foundation but high up off the ground and had never flooded until last summer, the summer when Dex and Amber were here. Both of them had nearly lost their lives in that flood, but thankfully they were okay.

Bunk beds were in three of the bedrooms. He counted six beds. But he also counted six names on the doors. Apparently the Joneses assigned each bed and put the boys' names on the doors. He rather sourly wondered if that was so they'd remember the kids' names as they funneled child after child through here. From what Silver had told him, Eddie had never felt loved here.

But then again, Eddie was probably hard to love because he got into so much trouble. So maybe it wasn't fair to just assume the foster parents didn't care about the kids in their care. After all, once he and Silver had broken the news about Eddie to Mrs. Jones, she'd broken down. And she'd sent the other boys to a neighbor's house down the road until she could compose herself. She didn't want them seeing her cry and worrying, or at least that was what she'd said.

Still, what he was seeing with the bedrooms, and the number of kids he'd counted when they arrived, had him heading back into the living room to ask a question.

Mrs. Jones kept staring straight in front of her as if preoccupied with her sad thoughts, but she'd dried her tears by now and was quietly talking to Silver. They sat beside each other on the couch, holding hands like old friends. He paused in the doorway, admiring Silver once again for the way she seemed to truly care about others and want to help them, even if they didn't deserve it. He knew she didn't like the woman she was comforting, and yet he could see the compassion in her expression, in the way she held the other woman's hand and spoke to her.

Silver was a truly special woman, and he was getting deeper and deeper in this. What had he been thinking to offer to take her to his apartment tonight?

She glanced up at him and gave him a watery smile. She must have cried right along with Mrs. Jones.

He returned her smile and headed into the room, taking a seat across from them on a brown leather recliner. "Mrs. Jones, I noticed there are six boys here and six bunk beds. Where did Eddie sleep?"

She glanced off into space before waving her hand, the wadded-up tissue in it flopping as she did. "Oh, he moved out on his birthday. I mean, he still came home for dinner and such. But he wanted his own space. He couldn't afford anything yet, so we let him move into the tree house out back."

"Tree house?"

She had the grace to blush. "Yes. I know it sounds bad, but honestly, the tree house is just about as nice as this house inside. Tony built it years ago when we realized we were going to end up taking in middle-school-aged kids. He thought it would be fun to have a big tree house for them and even hooked up a bathroom of sorts, with real running water and a pipe that connects to the septic system." She patted the corners of her eyes. "Eddie loved that tree house. He spent a lot of time there. I couldn't tell him no when he begged to move out there."

"If it's okay, I'd like to see it," he said.

She looked off into space again. "Of course, of course. You do whatever you need to do, Officer. And if there's something I can do to help your investigation, let me know. Tony will be devastated when he hears about Eddie."

Silver exchanged a startled glance with Colton, who only shrugged. What Mrs. Jones had just said didn't jibe at all with the way that Eddie had portrayed his foster parents. But where Silver probably believed everything Eddie had ever told her, Colton was more inclined to think that maybe Eddie had exaggerated. There certainly wasn't anything about this house, or in how the other foster kids had acted when they got here, to make him think they weren't well taken care of or that the Joneses didn't care about them.

Eddie had been a teenager, and life through the eyes of a teenager, especially a troubled one, could often be very different from the reality of those around them.

Silver rose from the couch along with Mrs. Jones. "Will you be okay if I go with Detective Graham to look at the tree house?"

"Of course, of course. I'm going to head on up to Betty's to see the boys. You've been very sweet to me this evening, Silver. You didn't have to be, either, so I want you to know that I appreciate it. You and I have never said more than a few words to each other, but I've always admired you."

Silver blinked in obvious surprise. "You do?"

She nodded. "You went to college and worked

hard for everything that you have. And you've never been anything but nice to me. I appreciate that. Thank you for being Eddie's friend, too. I know you tutored him and helped him out. Not that Eddie ever said anything about it. I heard from others what was going on." She swiped at her wet eyes again. "Eddie and I didn't always see eye to eye. It does my heart good to know he had you as a friend when I couldn't be that for him."

Silver hugged the other woman, and the three of them left the house, with Elisa Jones hurrying up the road toward the house where she'd sent the boys and Colton and Silver heading around to the back of the property.

"You okay?" Colton asked.

"I guess I'm…confused." She shrugged. "Maybe I misjudged her all this time."

He didn't know what to say to that, so he didn't say anything. She'd have to work through this one on her own.

In spite of what Mrs. Jones had said about the

tree house being nice, Colton hadn't expected it to be *this* nice. A good fifty yards from the house, it was about fifteen feet off the ground, with a massive deck circling around it, snugged up against the tree trunk. A system of steel supports beneath it went all the way to the ground, preserving the health of the tree by not impaling it, but also providing the strength needed to keep the heavy contraption from falling down.

Arched over a split in the main trunk, the actual "house" part of it was about the size of a bedroom, with windows on two sides and a full-sized door on the front. Silver and Colton climbed the steel ladder and he helped her step out onto the deck.

"This is one heck of a tree house," he said. "But I suppose it makes sense. Drew said that Mr. Jones is an engineer. This was probably a pet project, to use his skills from work in addition to making something the boys would enjoy."

Silver ran her hand along the railing, her face

a mask of awe and pleasure. "It's beautiful. I love that he used real branches to build the railing system. And the forest is gorgeous up here. What a view."

Colton couldn't help smiling to see her joy in something as simple as a view. He loved how she appreciated the simple things that most people missed. The view was amazing, even though most of it was of other trees, too thick to reveal much of the surrounding canals and swamps. But he was more interested right now in the heavy vines hanging down on all sides from the branches above. Instead of twining around the tree trunk, they'd been cut free to swing like thick ropes. He reached out and grabbed one of them and yanked. Solid, sturdy, easy to hold on to because of the offshoots and holes nature automatically built into the vine. He looked down at the railing in front of him. And then at the next tree over, which also had thick vines hanging down.

"Huh. I'll be."

"What? Did you find something?" Silver rushed over to him, her eyebrows drawn down.

He held up the vine and pointed to the railing. "See how that top rail is scuffed and scarred? And how that tree over there has more vines hanging down?"

Her eyes widened. "What are you thinking? Surely Eddie didn't stand on the railing and swing on that vine as if he were Tarzan or something."

"I'd be willing to bet that he did. And from the way this railing is scarred up, he did it a lot."

She shaded her eyes from the setting sun that was peeking through the branches. "That's a scary thought. We're a long ways up. One wrong step or one mistimed grab and it would be all over."

"Yeah, but it's also genius. If someone was after you and you could get up in the trees without them seeing you, boom, you're gone. A quiet getaway with no one the wiser."

"I suppose so. But that gives me hives just

thinking about it. Someone could have been killed." She grimaced and exchanged a solemn look with him, silently acknowledging that someone *had* been killed—Eddie. Just not while he was swinging from the vines.

He squeezed her shoulder. "Wait here. I'll go in first, make sure there aren't any critters inside."

She shivered. "Be my guest. I don't want to come face-to-face with a raccoon or, worse, a bat."

He swung open the door. A guttural shout sounded from just inside.

"Colton, look out!" Silver yelled.

He swore and threw his arms up to block the man lunging at him with a knife.

Chapter Thirteen

Silver clawed for her gun. Colton twisted his attacker's wrist, and the knife clattered to the deck. Colton pivoted and rolled, throwing the other man against the railing. He let out a cry of pain just as Silver brought her gun up.

That blond hair. That youthful face. Oh, no.

Colton drew his fist back.

"No, stop!" Silver yelled as she holstered her gun. "It's Charlie."

Colton hesitated, his fist still raised. Charlie jerked to the side, rolled out from under him and ran for the railing.

"Oh no, you don't," Colton growled as he

jumped to his feet. He ran and dove for Charlie just as the boy grabbed a vine and shoved off the top railing.

Silver gasped and covered her mouth in horror as the young man fell several feet. Then the vine jerked as he caught a good handhold, and it swung him toward the other tree. A flash of white tennis shoes as Charlie grabbed another vine and pushed off the other side of the tree and he was gone.

Colton grabbed the vine by the tree house and looked as though he was considering going after him. Silver jumped between him and the railing and held her hands out to stop him.

"Wait. It's too dangerous. You could fall. And besides, we don't know why Charlie was here or what he was doing. As much as I hate to admit it, it could be a trap."

His jaw muscle worked as he stared at the other tree. He'd climbed more than a few in his day and even swung from a few, courtesy of a well-hewn rope. Vines couldn't be that much harder and might even be easier to use because of so many handholds. But if Charlie had been watching them and scrambled up into the tree house to lure him into chasing him, it could very well be a trap.

He dropped the vine and stepped back. "Okay, you're right." He scooped up the knife Charlie had left behind, a six-inch blade with a serrated edge. "This is a heck of a knife. He meant business. I don't think we have to wonder whose side he's on. Definitely not ours." He hiked his leg up on the railing and yanked back his jeans, then carefully secured the knife inside his boot.

"You're right," Silver said. "I shouldn't have interfered. It's just that he's so young, and I was afraid you'd hurt him. But *you* could have been hurt, or worse. I'm so, so sorry."

His face softened as he straightened. "Your idiot former boss is right about one thing— you're softhearted. But he's wrong to think that's a weakness." He cupped her face and pressed a gentle kiss against her lips. "Don't ever change, Silver Westbrook."

She stood there in shock as he drew his pistol, then made a textbook entrance into the tree house, searching for intruders of the two-foot variety even though he'd teased her about the four-foot kind. He was doing his job, exactly as he should, while she'd failed miserably in that department.

Distracting him while he was fighting someone was inexcusable and went against her training. But seeing that young face had reminded her of Eddie, and the horrible way that he'd died, beaten to death. And she'd just...reacted.

She shivered and rubbed her hands up and down her arms. Crying out for Colton to stop was wrong, and dangerous. And yet he wasn't even upset with her. That kind of understanding and forgiveness was so foreign to her she wasn't sure that she understood it. And she certainly didn't deserve it.

"Clear," he called out from inside the tree house. "You can come in."

Determined to do better—for Colton's sake, and hers—she scanned the trees around them. Then she looked below, from every angle. When she didn't see any signs of intruders, she headed inside.

The tree trunk came up through the middle of the room, making it a doughnut shape with more than three feet of clearance all around the tree. A tiny sink and full-size toilet sat on one side. A microwave and dorm-sized refrigerator formed a kitchen. And an air mattress with a pillow and quilt thrown on top must have been where Eddie slept when he was here.

"I wonder what Charlie was doing in here," she said.

He was currently kneeling on the floor, looking at an old trunk beside the air mattress. He waved at a trash can off to the side, full of plastic wrappers from candy bars and the kinds of sandwiches that came from a machine, along with a mound of empty water bottles. "Looks like he was camping out. He was supposed to have left with his parents, right? Maybe he ran away?"

"He must have. I wonder why. I hope they weren't abusing him or something. Sad."

"I suppose it's possible, but he didn't look abused. No bruises or cuts. Then again, I know that stuff doesn't always show, especially if it's psychological abuse."

"No," she said softly. "And that can be the worst kind." She hugged her arms around her middle.

Colton's head shot up. "You sound like you speak from personal experience."

She thought about denying it, but this was Colton. And although she'd never talked about her troubled past with anyone, she knew she could talk to him about it. He wouldn't judge her or make her feel ashamed. "Yes. I speak from personal experience."

He started to rise, but she waved him back down.

"I'm fine. No reason to go over that, certainly not now. But thank you for caring. I can see it in your eyes."

"Silver, if you want to talk—"

"I know. Thank you. Not now."

He hesitated, looking uncertain.

She knelt beside him and kissed him, then waved at the trunk. "What are you doing?"

He searched her eyes, as if undecided.

"Colton, it was a very long time ago. I'm fine. The trunk?"

He frowned at her, and she loved that he was so concerned. But he finally turned back to the trunk. "It's the only thing in here that's locked up and I want to know why. I couldn't find a key anywhere." He pulled his knife from his boot and went to work on the wood surrounding the lock. It popped off and the top sprang open. "Looks mostly like clothes. And books."

Silver helped him sort through everything,

smiling sadly when she found the algebra book with notes in it that she'd made while helping Eddie pass his final.

"Aha." Colton held up a small key. "This looks promising. If we can figure out what it goes to." He ran his hands along the bottom underneath the clothes, then sat back. "I don't think there's anything else in here, though. So the key must be what he wanted to keep safe."

"It kind of looks like a padlock key, or maybe it's to another trunk," she said. "I suppose we could ask Mrs. Jones where he might keep more belongings, in case there's a trunk there."

He helped her to her feet and soon they were back on solid ground. She'd just turned toward the path that led to the house when he tugged her hand.

"I'm pretty sure there isn't anything in that house where the key would fit. I searched it pretty thoroughly earlier. But we can check out that path over there." He pointed off into the trees. "If you'll notice, it follows the direction where Charlie went, and it appears well-worn, like maybe Eddie went there a lot. I for one would like to know where it goes. And the sun is going down. I'd rather do it while we have daylight left, especially if there's some evidence out here that Charlie might be in the process of making disappear. I'd hate to come out here tomorrow with Drew and a team and find out we'd just missed a big score that would crack the case wide open. Are you game?"

"You bet I am. Let's go."

After a good fifteen-minute walk, the path abruptly ended in a clearing, not all that far from the tree house—maybe about a few hundred yards. And in the middle was a dilapidated-looking wooden shed that was about twenty-by-twenty, with rotting boards. It would have looked abandoned and unused if it weren't for the shiny metal door affixed to the front, and what was hanging off the metal loop. A padlock.

"Do you see what I see?" Colton asked.

"A place for our key."

They searched the woods in the immediate vicinity of the shed, but it was all clear, so they headed back to the shed, key in hand.

Silver took out her gun, scanning the clearing while he tried the key.

Click.

"Bingo," he said. He took the lock off, flipped back the latch and pulled out his pistol. "Wait until I give the all clear."

She nodded, keeping guard while he went inside. A few seconds later, a low whistle sounded from inside.

"Jackpot," he said. "You'll want to see this."

When she stepped through the doorway, Colton held up his phone, using the flashlight app to show her what he'd found. Nearly every inch of space along the walls was taken up with three-foot-high stacks of something beneath heavy green tarps. And since Colton had flipped back the tarp closest to the door, she didn't have to guess what was underneath.

Bricks of cocaine. Dozens of them. No, hundreds based on the number of stacks.

"This is worse than anything I ever imagined. If Eddie did anything to make the dealer feel threatened, no wonder he killed him. This is worth millions on the street."

He flipped off the light on his phone and tried to make a call. "No signal. No surprise." He shoved the phone into the holder on this waist. "We're getting out of here. Now."

They turned around, but suddenly Colton put his hand over her mouth and hauled her back inside. "We're too late," he whispered next to her ear. "Listen."

Voices, two men and a woman, sounded from outside, approaching fast.

He moved his hand and pulled out his knife.

"What are you doing?" she whispered. "We have to get out of the shed."

"Nowhere to go without them hearing us. Hurry, get under that tarp at the far end."

"Should I close the door?"

"No. We can't lock it from inside." He threw a tarp up near the door, pulled out his knife, and slashed and tore several jagged holes inside the top brick, spilling white powder all over the floor.

He shoved the knife back into his boot and grabbed her hand. "Hurry."

Shouts sounded from outside in the clearing as she and Colton scrambled over one of the stacks and slid into the tight space next to the wall. He threw the tarp over the top of both of them and they both pulled their guns out, waiting, listening, barely breathing for fear of making any sound.

She wanted to ask him why he'd cut open that brick of cocaine, but she couldn't for fear of someone hearing. Because the sound of footsteps told her that whoever was outside had just stepped into the shed.

"What the hell?" a man's voice shouted. "You didn't lock the door?"

"Of course I locked it," another man said. "Someone must have busted in."

"Yeah, I'll tell you who got in. A rat, or maybe a raccoon. Because you forgot to lock the place. Look at that mess. It tore open one of the bricks."

"For the last time, I didn't forget."

"Tell that to Cato and see what he says."

Silver drew in a sharp breath. Colton put a hand on her shoulder in warning. She hoped they hadn't heard her, but she was so surprised to hear them say Cato's name. So he was involved. But how deep? Could he be the leader they'd been looking for? Somehow she couldn't picture him as the head of a multimillion-dollar operation.

Footsteps crossed farther into the shed. The sound of vinyl sliding against vinyl came from just a few feet of their hiding place. One of the men had thrown back a tarp. "Everything else looks untouched."

"Of course it does," the first man's voice said,

sounding as though he thought the other man was an idiot. "The rodent got high and went off to die somewhere. If a person had done this, he wouldn't have wasted anything. He'd have made off with our stash."

Another tarp was flipped up, the air whispering against the one where she and Colton were hiding. She tightened both hands around her gun. Colton's left hand touched her right wrist, applying gentle, steady pressure, forcing her to lower the gun just a few inches. It was his silent way of letting her know not to panic. She swallowed hard and focused on her breathing, in, out, in, out, all through the mouth. No noise.

"Bring her in here," the first man ordered.

The man who'd flipped back the tarps covered the stacks again, or at least that was what Silver guessed he was doing based on the vinyl sounds.

Her mind raced, wondering who "her" was. Did they have a hostage?

"Mrs. Jones," the first man said. "You been in the shed?"

Mrs. Jones? Silver's hands tightened on her gun again. How could she? Eddie had died, and she'd been a part of this all along.

"No, no, no, sir. I don't even have a key. Eddie had the key."

"See?" the man said. "I told you, raccoon. 'Cause Eddie sure ain't comin' in here anymore." He laughed at his own joke.

"That's a terrible thing to say," Mrs. Jones said, her voice shaking with fear and anger both. "Why would you kill that boy? We've done everything you asked us to do."

What was she talking about? Had she made some kind of deal?

"I'm not the one who killed him. But I tell you what, I can take you to the boss, let you ask him directly if you want."

The cruelty in his voice had bile rising in Silver's throat. Colton's shoulder brushed against hers, and she could feel the tension in his body.

He was just as angry as she was. And there was more to Mrs. Jones's situation than Silver had guessed. She definitely didn't seem to be a willing participant in the drug operation.

"What about my Tony? You said you'd let him go. Where is he?"

"Hold your horses. He's fine, just like we promised. As long as you ain't told no one about us?"

"No, no, like I said. We've done everything you asked."

"You did just fine, Mrs. Jones. Now, we've heard there might be a couple of cops in town, a man and a woman. You know anything about that?"

There was a pause, then, "Yes, they were at my house. They told me about Eddie. But I didn't tell them anything. I sent them away."

"You sure about that? You sure you didn't tell them anything?" His voice sounded menacing again.

"I swear, as God is my witness. Please, you're hurting my arm."

"Well, I'm sorry about that, Mrs. Jones. There, now, all better?"

"I'm fine," she said. "I always do what you ask. I meet you here every night to check in."

"And we appreciate that, don't we, Jack?"

A noncommittal grunt was the only sign that the other man was still there.

"Tell you what," the obvious leader of the duo said. "You don't even have to meet us out here tomorrow. We'll give you a night off, for good behavior. But we'll still be watching you, to make sure you aren't talking to anyone that you shouldn't."

"I don't need a night off. I need to see Tony. It's time to let him and the others go. Like you promised. You were supposed to let them go after the last shipment."

"We're running behind schedule. *This* is the last shipment. We have to wait until the weekend to bring the barge around or we'll attract attention. Just a few more days and this will all be over." His voice sounded placating now. "You run on back to the house and keep those cops out of our hair. And just as soon as that barge is loaded, we'll let Mr. Jones and the others go."

"You promise?" she said. "You give me your word? You won't hurt Tony?"

"You have my word, Mrs. Jones. As long as I have yours that you aren't going to tell anyone."

"I haven't told a soul. And I won't."

"Good, good. Now run along."

The sound of her hurrying out of the shed and into the clearing gradually faded.

"What were you talking about?" the second man said. "This is our last shipment?"

He laughed. "Not even close. This place has been a gold mine for us. Not a single lost kilo, until that stupid critter got in here. No, we're going to be here for a long time to come. We just have to clean up a few messes, and make sure all the leaks are plugged. Starting with Tony. Once that's all taken care of, and the shipment is on its way, then we'll have to arrange some kind of accident for Mrs. Jones. And next time you have to go, go in your pants, dude. No leaving your post until it's time for the next guard. We'll be lucky if Cato or the boss doesn't take the price of that ruined kilo out of our take as it is. Now keep an eye on the place. Can you do that?"

They stepped out of the shed arguing and the door slammed shut. The padlock clicked, and the sound of footsteps moved away, but only one set. The man who'd gotten in trouble for leaving the shed was still outside, standing guard.

"We're trapped," Silver whispered next to Colton's ear.

"Not for long. Stay here."

"But—"

"Wait for me. Don't come out until I tell you." He threw back the tarp and climbed over the stack of cocaine bricks they'd hidden behind, then flipped it back over her.

She fisted her hands, hating that he hadn't

given her a chance to even discuss whatever plan he had.

A light shuffling noise sounded near the door, then a scratching sound like claws on wood. Oh, no. Was there a rat in here?

The shuffling and scratching started again, and the door rattled in its frame as though something was pushing against it. Silver shivered with revulsion, thinking about the animal doing that. And where was Colton? What was he doing?

Scratch. Thump.

Cursing sounded from outside. The padlock rattled against the door and then the door flew open.

"All right, you little rodent. Where are you hiding?"

Another loud thump sound. Then a crack. A loud groan. Then nothing.

"You can come out now," Colton called out.

Silver threw the tarp off and blinked in surprise. A man lay facedown on the dirt, eyes closed.

"Well, I'll be," she said. "I guess the rodent's name was Colton. Pretty slick."

"We'll tie him up and leave him in here. Mind pulling his shoelaces out of his shoes? We can tie his hands behind his back with those and save my handcuffs in case we need them later."

While she did as he'd asked, he used his knife to cut long strips from the man's shirt and then gagged and bound him so he couldn't cry out.

When they were done, he was trussed up like a turkey for Thanksgiving, still unconscious on the floor.

Last, Colton took the man's gun, then waved Silver out of the shed so he could lock it again.

"We don't have any way of knowing what time another guard will come to relieve him. We need to get out of here."

They hurried into the cover of trees. Silver stopped when she realized Colton wasn't following her. He stood staring back at the clearing and the trees surrounding it.

Her stomach dropped with dread. "Is another guard coming already?"

"I don't think so." They both kept their voices low so they wouldn't carry. His intense gaze bored into her. "What did you make out of their conversation with Mrs. Jones? That they've got hostages, right? Tony is Mr. Jones. And she mentioned others."

"You're thinking we should try to free them, aren't you? Instead of going for help?"

He shook his head. "No. I'm thinking *I* should try to free them, and *you* should go for help."

She put her hands on her hips. "If you think for one minute that I'm going to leave you to face them alone, you're seriously deluded. No way. Where you go, I go. I'm your wingman. I've got your back."

His jaw tightened and he strode toward her. If she hadn't already met him and known how kind and honorable he was, she'd have been intimidated by his deep scowl and flashing blue eyes. As it was, he was still a bit intimidating as he glared down at her.

"I'm all about equal rights and respect for women and not trying to impose false limitations on them," he said, "but this is one time when I'm going to be a complete chauvinist. You are *not* going with me."

"I'm an officer of the law, just like you. We've got the same training. I'm armed and a pretty good shot. Why *wouldn't* I go with you?"

He backed her up against a tree and tilted her chin up. "I can't risk something happening to you. And besides, it makes more sense for one of us to go for help. You can head to the interstate, call Drew, have him send the cavalry. Once I locate where they've got the hostages, I'll do some kind of diversion, hold them off until you bring help. It's a good plan."

She rolled her eyes. "It's a terrible plan. Two guns are better than one any day. And the idea of a diversion is to have one person create the diversion while the other does whatever needs to be done. It doesn't make sense for you to try to do both."

He started to say something else, but she pressed her fingers against his lips, stopping him. "I appreciate that you care about me. Trust me. The feeling is mutual. I don't want anything to happen to you any more than you want something happening to me. But I'm just as stubborn as you, maybe more so, and there's no way you're going to make me abandon you. Standing here arguing about it is just wasting time. If you want to try to save the hostages, then you'll have to accept my help, or keep looking over your shoulder the whole time. Because that's where I'll be, behind you, watching out for you, covering you. We're partners in this. And that's what partners do."

He pulled her hand down from his mouth. "You are the most frustrating female I've ever met."

She slid her hands up behind his neck and

pressed her body against his. "Shut up and kiss me so we can get on with this."

His mouth swooped down and covered hers in a wild, almost savage kiss that had her toes curling in her shoes. And then, before she could even catch her breath, he grabbed her hand and tugged her behind him in an all-out run in the same direction where they'd heard the gunman go earlier.

Chapter Fourteen

Their light was fading fast. Silver was amazed that Colton had been able to track the second gunman at all with what little light they'd had. He was obviously an experienced tracker, which opened up all kinds of interesting questions to ask him someday about his past—if she ever got that opportunity. But even Colton didn't seem to know which way their prey had gone now.

He knelt on the trail they'd been following, pressing his fingers against the soil, feeling for the ridges that would indicate a footprint.

"What about using your flashlight app?" Silver asked. "I can cup my hands around it to try to keep anyone from seeing the light while you get a quick look and try to find more shoe prints."

He considered it, then shook his head. "Too risky. One flash of light seen by the wrong person and suddenly we're surrounded." He stood and brushed off his hands on his jeans. "We'll have to make an educated guess. We know they went this way. From here, there are only two places where the brush is thin enough and the ground firm enough to make for easy travel—that northeast area up by that big oak, and this more westerly turn near that fallen log."

"So we split up?"

"No way. We choose one or the other, together, and see where it goes. If, after a few minutes, we can't pick up the trail again, we'll backtrack and try the other one."

"You're taking this chauvinist thing really far."

"You knew how I felt before we started out. You ready to turn back and ride for help?"

"If I thought I could get help in time to really help, I would. But you and I both know that by the time we could get someone out here, whatever plans those gunmen had for the hostages could be over. No, our only chance to save them is to work together and keep going forward."

He scrubbed his jaw and studied both potential paths. "Northeast?"

"That's the way I'd go. Seems firmer, drier. I'm surprised we haven't seen anyone else out here. Leaving one man to guard a shed full of merchandise doesn't seem very smart."

"I agree. But you heard what they said about the hostages and cleaning up messes. Maybe whoever else is out here is helping with whatever is planned for the hostages."

"Then we need to find them, fast. Let's go."

They continued along the path, looking out for bent or broken branches, or footprints, in the dirt. But with the sun almost completely set, their only light was from the rising moon. And it wasn't even a full moon.

He suddenly held up a hand, signaling for her to stop, then pressed his finger against his mouth for her to be quiet. She paused beside him, listening, trying to hear whatever he'd heard. And then she heard it—the low murmur of voices, muted, as if coming from far away. It was hard to tell in the woods just how far because of the way sound carried out here.

He motioned again for silence, then crept forward. She followed, and together they made their way, getting closer and closer to the sounds they were hearing. After they had maneuvered around a particularly thick mass of fallen limbs and soggy ground to find solid ground again, the glow of lights had them ducking down. But the lights weren't moving. They were steady, and coming from what appeared to be a large clearing at least half a football field away.

Colton reached back for her hand and tugged her with him behind an enormous, twisted cypress, its knobby knees pushing up out of the brackish water of the encroaching swamp on its southern side. She and Colton crouched behind the opposite side, blocking them from the light.

"There could be guards out here in the woods," Colton whispered. "I'll circle around, try to pinpoint how many there are and where they're stationed. If I see the hostages, I'll get a count and the lay of the land, see what we're up against. Then we'll brainstorm the best way to proceed."

She grabbed his hand as he started to turn away. "Promise me you won't try to take on these guys all by yourself. Promise me you'll come back and we'll do this, whatever we decide to do, *together*."

He framed her face in his hands and pressed a fierce kiss against her lips. "Together," he whispered.

And then he was gone.

COLTON CREPT THROUGH the woods, skirting around thick mud bogs and sharp palmettos, carefully making his way in a circle around the source of the light, which he presumed to be the drug dealers' base camp.

He hated lying to Silver, but if the situation was as dangerous as he expected, no way was he going to come back and bring her with him. Not because he didn't think she was capable. She was DEA and had probably faced worse before. But he'd bet everything he owned that she'd faced it with a team of agents at her side. Because no one in their right mind would try to take on a group of heavily armed mercenary types and thugs that typically made up drug-running operations. And that included him, at any other time. But tonight everything was different.

Because of Silver.

She was one of those rare people who believed in the inherent good in people, in spite of the job she had and the evil she must have seen on a nearly daily basis just as he did. And she'd already suffered such incredible loss when Eddie was killed. He couldn't bear to see her hurting like that again if more innocents were killed. So, knowing it was virtually impossible for Drew to round up the troops to save the hostages in time, here he was, risking everything to try to do the impossible himself.

As he made his way around a large group of palmettos to finally get a clear view of what he was up against, his only real hope was that it wasn't as bad as he'd feared.

Nope. It was worse, far worse.

A large tent sat at one side of the clearing, with at least ten feet of cleared space between it and any foliage, making it nearly impossible to approach without being seen. As Colton watched, three armed men stepped out of the woods and went into the tent. Four armed guards walked the perimeter of the clearing, each with a semi-automatic rifle strapped over his shoulder. And lighting all of it up were three clusters of bright lights, powered by generators.

At the other end of the clearing sat two combat-style heavy-duty Jeeps, their drivers armed with the same type of semiautomatic rifles. Arms crossed and looking bored, they appeared to be waiting for someone or something. Silver had been right. Something was definitely going on.

And he was pretty sure that "something" had to do with the four men bound and gagged in the middle of the clearing, inside a cage. Correction, *one man*, and three *boys*—Eddie's age, around nineteen or twenty. Counting the drivers in the Jeeps, the hostages were guarded by at least nine heavily armed men, ten if he counted the other guard back at the shed, who could come running if needed.

Yeah, this was way worse than he'd hoped.

A whisper of sound from above had him diving to the side and whipping out his knife just as a man leaped down at him from a tree branch. He scrambled to roll away. Colton tackled him and jumped on his back, shoving the man's face into the mud so he couldn't cry out. He held his knife at the ready, grabbed a fistful of the man's hair and yanked his head up to draw his knife across his throat. He'd just reached his blade around to end it when he heard a whimper.

Like what a child might make. *Or a terrified teenager.*

Colton held the knife against the man's throat and leaned down to get a good look at his face. *Charlie.* Ah, hell. He lightened the pressure of the blade. "Give me one good reason not to kill you right now."

"We…we could have…we could have killed *you*," he blubbered, barely able to get coherent words past his lips. "But we didn't."

"We?" He pressed the knife harder against Charlie's throat.

Charlie thumped one of his hands against the ground. Branches crackled overhead. Colton swore and yanked Charlie up out of the mud, pulling him in front of him as he scooted back against a tree, knife still held to the teenager's throat. He whipped out his pistol, aiming it at the six other young men who'd just dropped from the sky and now crouched in front of him as if ready to pounce. But, in spite of Charlie's claims about them killing him, the boys had no weapons, at least none that Colton saw.

"Back up, or he dies," Colton ordered, leveling his pistol at the nearest boy while holding the knife steady against Charlie's throat.

"Do as he says," Charlie whispered, his voice hoarse, barely audible.

The boys slowly raised their hands in the air and backed up several steps. Moonlight slanted down through the branches overhead, illuminating some of their faces. And that was when Colton recognized them. They were the foster kids whom Mrs. Jones had sent to a neighbor's house when he and Silver arrived to break the news about Eddie's death. But how had they ended up here?

A quick glance up confirmed that there were vines hanging from the trees above, the vines these boys had used to swing from tree to tree and sneak up on him, then drop down like ninjas. He couldn't help being impressed.

He slowly lowered his gun, pointing it at the ground, and eased the knife a few inches away from Charlie's throat.

"All right." He kept his voice low so the gunmen back by the tents wouldn't hear him. "You've got my attention. Start talking."

THERE SHOULD HAVE been a trench in the dirt by now for all the pacing that Silver had done. She strode back and forth between the same two trees with her pistol out, hanging down by her thigh toward the ground. How long had it been since Colton had left? Twenty minutes? Thirty? More? Certainly enough for him to have performed reconnaissance and returned.

Unless he'd lied about coming back for her and them rescuing the hostages together.

A whisper of air stirred her hair against her neck. But there didn't seem to be a breeze. She lifted her gun, panning it back and forth, but she didn't see anything.

"Colton?" she whispered. "Is that you?"

"Silver, put your gun away."

She frowned. "Colton?" She turned around. "Where are you?"

"Look up."

She lifted her head, and her mouth fell open in shock. "What are you...how did you—"

"The gun?"

"Oh, sorry." She shoved it into her waistband and moved back.

He let go of the vine he was hanging from and dropped to the ground, rolled and then jumped to his feet. Before she could ask him what was going on, he grabbed her and pulled her back against the trunk of a tree.

Thump, thump, thump. Several more men dropped from the sky near where Colton had been a moment before. By the time he let her go, she counted six, no, seven young men, *young* being the operative word, standing there staring at her. She frowned as she studied their faces, and then it dawned on her who they were.

"You're all Mrs. Jones's kids. And…is that you, Charlie?"

The blond boy moved from the rear of the group to the front. "Yes, ma'am. I hope we didn't scare you. We're on your side. I mean, you and Detective Graham's side."

She pressed her hand against her chest where her heart seemed to want to burst through her ribs. She'd had quite a fright and wasn't sure what to think. Obviously, these boys weren't a threat or Colton wouldn't have led them here. And he didn't have his gun out. But, then, why were they here? And what did they want?

"Colton, what's going on? Were these young men taken hostage?" She put her hands on her hips. "Did you risk your life and rescue them all on your own? You promised me you wouldn't—"

"Whoa, whoa, now." He held out his hands in a placating gesture. "One question at a time.

No, I didn't rescue anyone. And no, these young men weren't hostages—not this week anyway."

She frowned. "What do you mean, this week?"

"Charlie, tell her what you told me."

She listened with growing horror as he recounted his tale, explaining how it had all started because Eddie and some others were being bullied by a kid at school who acted as if the fact that his parents were rich meant he was important and they were beneath him. One of the boys got a hold of some liquor from his older brother and passed it around as they griped about the snobby boy. Then, on a drunken dare, Eddie and some of the others decided to break into the kid's house when no one was home and trash the place.

And that was exactly what they did. But they also found something at the house, a kilo of cocaine and a stash of money, thousands of dollars. If they'd been sober, they'd have thought it through. But they were high and mad and took the drugs and the money.

"Wait," Silver said. "Are you saying the man you stole from was a drug dealer?"

"Yes, ma'am. But we didn't realize it. I mean, we were kind of wasted or we'd have known that we should have hightailed it out of there as soon as we found the drugs."

"Let me guess. He had you on surveillance video? And knew you were local high school kids?"

Charlie nodded. "He threatened to tell the police, show them the video of us breaking in. He said no one would believe us about the drugs being his. That our only chance was to do some favors for him."

"The burglary ring," she said, finally understanding how it had started.

"No," Colton corrected her. "The robberies came later. The man they crossed was a low guy on the totem pole in the drug world. A lowlife who's already been arrested on other charges. I recognized his name when Charlie gave me the details. But before his arrest, he told his boss about the break-in, and his boss sent some thugs to rough up the kids and said they had to work off their debt."

She nodded. "Debt meaning they owed the dealer for double-crossing his organization, even though they didn't realize they were doing it."

"Yes, ma'am," Charlie said. "We gave him the kilo and cash, but he still said we owed him. He threatened to kill us, or the Joneses, if we didn't do what he said."

"Which was what? Running drugs for him?"

"Basically. He needed a location where the cops wouldn't be looking for a drug operation and thought he could use Mystic Glades with us guiding them through the canals and covering for him, warning him if things got hot."

Another boy stepped forward. "We didn't know what to do, so we told Mr. Jones. But we were being watched and didn't know it. Two men busted in the door and took him away, along with me and Todd." He waved at the boy beside him.

"But, what, you escaped? Both of you? But Mr. Jones is still a hostage?"

"No, ma'am. They knew social services might get involved if we went missing. So he let us go but kept Mr. Jones. But then Eddie got the idea that he could buy us out of this mess. That's when he started the burglary ring. We were trying to get enough money that the dealer would leave us alone and let Mr. Jones go."

"Remember Ron Dukes?" Colton asked her. She nodded.

"He was the brains of that operation, a genius with security alarms. So they enlisted him to help."

"Wait, then Ron was...he wasn't working with the dealer?"

"No. He wanted to help Eddie and the others buy their freedom."

"Oh, my God. And he paid for it with his life."

"No, ma'am. Ron is one of the hostages."

She blinked in confusion.

Colton took her hands in his and gave her a sympathetic grin. "It's a lot to take in all at once. That bleach we saw at the garbage facility was just that, bleach. It had nothing to do with Ron or anyone else, as far we know. But, basically, what happened is that Eddie and the others got mixed up in the drugs by accident. And they tried to buy their way out of it by stealing things and selling them on the black market. What they didn't realize was that once you're in—"

"There's no way out," she said. "Believe me, I've seen that lesson over and over in my years as a DEA agent. So then Eddie, what, took the proceeds and tried to buy everyone's freedom?"

Colton nodded. "And he paid for it with his life."

She nodded, fighting back tears. "And the hostages are, what, insurance to make sure no one else pulls a stunt like Eddie did?"

"Yes, ma'am."

"Who killed him? I have to know."

"To answer that, we have to know who's running the whole operation."

She looked at Charlie. "I don't understand. All of you have to know who's calling the shots here."

"Cato's the head guy's right hand. We think he's the one who killed Eddie, too. But only because his boss told him to."

"Then who's his boss?"

Colton looked at the other boys and they all shrugged.

"We don't know. We've never seen him."

Silver shook her head in frustration.

"Silver," Colton said, "The hostages are in a small camp not far from here. It looks like they're about to be taken somewhere else. There's no reason to move them unless—"

"They're cleaning up," she whispered.

He nodded. "We can't wait any longer. We have to get them out of there."

"You said there was a camp. There are other gunmen there?"

"Ten, or more. With semiautomatic weapons."

She looked down at her pistol shoved into her waistband. Two guns, hers and Colton's—no, three, counting the handgun that Colton had taken off the guy in the shed. But that wasn't enough to take down ten armed men.

His hand gently pushed her chin up to look at him. "Hey. Don't give up already. This isn't over." He grinned and held up the key to the padlock. "The boys and I have a plan."

Chapter Fifteen

Colton held the keys to his Mustang out to Charlie, then hesitated. "Are you sure you know how to drive a stick?"

"Grew up on one. But I've never driven a 'Stang. That's gonna be sweet."

"Colton, we don't have time for this," Silver reminded him.

He winced as he dropped the keys in Charlie's hand. "All right, go. Be as quiet as you can. Assume Cato or his boss could have someone else out here in the woods looking for you. Don't take any chances. Once you get back to town, don't stop. We need real backup, cops, a SWAT team, not Freddie and her senior squad heading up here and getting themselves killed." He handed Charlie his phone. "Get to the interstate and press Send. The call is ready to go through to my boss. Tell him to send the cavalry."

"Got it."

"Go."

Charlie whirled around and disappeared into the woods.

"All right, to the shed. Come on." Colton took off at a run, with Silver and the boys trying to keep up with his long stride.

When they reached the shed, everyone stopped and Colton waved two of the boys forward.

"Okay, Ned—you're the one with the ciga-rette lighter, right?"

"Yes, sir."

"Good. You and Robert know what to do. Wait fifteen minutes to give us enough time to get in position. Then light it up. And, Ned? After this, you're giving up smoking. It's bad for you. Un-derstood?"

Ned grinned and gave Colton a salute. "Yes, sir."

"As soon as the fire catches, you climb a tree and make like Tarzan and get out of here. Got it?"

"Got it," they said in unison.

Colton returned Ned's salute and then eyed the rest of the group. "Okay, which of you juvenile delinquents has a pocketknife?"

Silver lightly punched him in the arm and he winked at her.

All three remaining boys raised their hands.

Colton cocked an eyebrow at Silver.

She rolled her eyes.

"All right. Special Agent Westbrook and I will do our part. Remember, only slash the tires on the rear Jeep. We'll need the other one to transport the hostages. Everyone ready?"

At their eager nods, he leaned down close to Silver. "Are *you* ready? If this doesn't go as planned, we'll be in a firefight for our lives, not to mention *their* lives." He motioned toward the boys.

"Let's do this."

They headed off in single file through the woods, following Colton's lead, stepping where he stepped. He really seemed to know what he was doing to not make much noise, avoiding twigs and anything that might alert the camp that they were coming.

When they reached the perimeter, they quietly made their way to the far side, where the Jeeps were parked.

Colton waved the boys over to a bush close to the first Jeep and gave them the thumbs-up signal. Then he and Silver circled through the woods toward the back middle of the camp and crouched down, opposite the cage where the hostages were sitting. Colton pulled out his knife. Silver drew her gun.

And then they waited.

And waited.

Colton was just about to suggest they go back to the shed to check on the boys when a flash of light speared through the night from that direction. Sparks rose in the air. The distant crackle of flames had the hostages turning to see what was happening.

One of the perimeter guards shouted, "Fire! It's coming from the direction of the shed. Come on."

To a man, the guards surged forward, including the ones in the tent and even the drivers, and ran toward the shed. Colton had based his plan on what would be more important to the head honcho and therefore to his men—the hostages or millions of dollars of cocaine. Money won every time.

But he was all too aware that it wouldn't take ten men to put out one little fire. They only had a few minutes, at best.

"Cover me," he told Silver.

She held her gun up, watching the other side of the camp for any returning guards.

Colton ran to the cage, his knife drawn. He hacked at the twine holding the door closed and then yanked it open.

"Hurry," Silver said. "I saw some kind of movement."

He ran inside and sliced the bindings on the hostages' legs but didn't bother with the hands.

"Come on," he said. "To the first Jeep. Run." He guided them out the door, but one of the boys had a hurt leg with a nasty cut. He winced when he tried to put weight on it. The boy was as tall as Colton and too heavy for him to carry. He pulled the boy's arm over his shoulder and helped him hobble to the Jeep.

When they got there, he settled him into the back. All the hostages were accounted for. And his prize tire slashers had done their job. The second Jeep's tires were all flat.

"Get in. Start the engine."

Shouts sounded behind him. He turned around to see two of the guards sprinting toward the encampment, guns drawn. He looked back at the Jeep, expecting Silver to be in it. She wasn't. He whirled around again. Silver wasn't by the tent. She wasn't in the Jeep. She wasn't anywhere.

"Silver?" he called out. "Silver?"

The crack of a bullet echoed through the woods. Colton dove down and brought up his gun, firing at the guard who'd shot at him. The guard catapulted back in a heap on the ground. The second guard took aim. Colton squeezed off two quick shots. The guard dove behind some bushes.

Colton thumped the back of the Jeep. "Go, go, go. Get out of here."

The man who Colton assumed was Mr. Jones hopped into the driver's seat. "Come on," he called out. "Get in."

"Not without Silver. Go. We'll catch up with you. Hurry before the rest of them come back."

Another bullet whined past him.

The Jeep took off, spitting up dirt and leaves as it barreled away.

Colton whirled around, ducking behind a tree as he looked everywhere for Silver. Where could she be? She should have been right behind him.

A scream sounded from off to his right some-where, galvanizing him into action. He fired two quick cover shots and took off, running as fast as he'd ever run in his life. *Please be okay, please be okay.*

Another scream.

Colton swore every curse word he knew.

Then he started praying.

His foot sank into a muddy bog and he fell hard, splashing face-first into some brackish water. He pushed himself upright and took off again. The sound of a powerful engine started up. He knew that sound. An airboat. He sprinted faster, pumping his legs up and down.

Moonlight flashed off the white hull of a boat, an airboat just up ahead. And on it he could see two figures, Silver and a tall, brawny man he'd fought with once before.

Cato.

The boat took off, speeding away from the makeshift dock.

There was no other boat.

Panic sent a burst of adrenaline straight through Colton. He put on a fresh burst of speed and leaped off the dock toward the airboat. He splashed into the marsh, then jerked forward. He managed to get one hand on the back of the boat, wedged in between the metal cage around the fan and the hull. The boat skipped and hopped over the shallows, slapping him around like a rag doll.

He struggled to hold on and finally got his other hand on the back of the boat. With the fan between him and the rest of the boat, Cato hadn't realized he was there. Silver sat on the floor of the boat at his feet, with Cato's gun pointed at her while he steered.

Colton gritted his teeth and fought inch over inch as he painstakingly clung to the boat and made his way up the side to get around the fan. The boat bumped across a mudflat, bouncing him up in the air. By some miracle he was flipped into the boat instead of into the marsh. He landed with a bone-jarring thud on the metal floor.

Cato and Silver both jerked their heads and looked at him.

His gun was long gone, lying somewhere on the bottom of the marsh. And he figured Silver's must have been taken, as well, or she'd already have figured out a way to shoot Cato.

He watched, seemingly in slow motion, as his fate played out in front of his eyes. Cato's gun began to swivel toward him. He knew the bullet would rip through him, killing him. It was impossible to miss at this range. He braced himself, feeling at peace, believing his sacrifice would give Silver the distraction she needed to save herself—to either push Cato overboard or jump over herself. She would survive. And that was all that mattered.

"No," he heard her scream.

Cato's gun jerked back toward her.

Colton launched himself at him, slamming his shoe against the other man's knee with a sickening crack as he delivered an uppercut to the underside of his arm, shoving the gun up toward the sky. The gun fired but then flew out of the boat, into the black marsh rushing by them at a dizzying speed.

Cato roared with rage, clutching his bad knee even as he struggled to remain upright by holding on to the wheel well.

Colton was about to punch him again when he looked past him and saw a black void rushing toward them. He shouted a warning and dove toward Silver, grabbing her around the waist and yanking her with him over the side of the boat. They plunged into the water, bottoming out on the muddy shallows.

A dull sound reverberated through the water and a fireball flashed its light above them. They broke the surface, bobbing like corks in the water as they stared at what was left of the airboat. It had run full speed into the upended roots of an enormous dead tree and had exploded on impact.

Colton grabbed Silver and hauled her to him, giving her a fierce hug. "I died inside when I couldn't find you back at the camp. And then I heard you scream."

"I'm sorry. I'm so sorry. He snuck up behind me."

He pulled her back and framed her face in his hands. "Are you okay?"

"I'm…" She looked down and wrinkled her nose in disgust. "Very dirty. And smelly. But yes, I'm fine."

"You smell wonderful to me." He kissed her until they were both breathless. Then they held hands, laughing as they struggled to find their footing in the shallow water and climb out onto the muddy bank.

Once they were on semidry land, they stood arm in arm watching the greedy fire licking at the wreckage and scorching the roots of the tree. Something white flashed in the water near the fire. A white shirt. Cato. He lay facedown in the water, his clothing ripped and burned.

Silver shivered against Colton and hugged him around the waist. "Please tell me the boys are okay. The hostages."

"Last I saw they were bouncing around in the back of the Jeep with Mr. Jones driving like his pants were on fire. And they were laughing, having the time of their lives. They should all be fine."

"Thank God." She let out a relieved breath. "Too bad we don't have a Jeep. Or a boat. I don't suppose you have a canoe hidden around here somewhere, do you?"

"Fresh out. How far do you suppose we are from town?"

"Let me put it this way. It's going to be a long night."

A loud hiss sounded from some tall grasses behind them. They jerked around.

"What was that?" Colton demanded.

"I think it was an alligator."

"You *think*?"

"Okay, *definitely* an alligator."

Another loud hiss sounded, along with what sounded like a low roar, closer, from their left.

Colton pulled her back toward the water. A splash sounded behind them, then another.

"Okay. This isn't looking good." A pair of green lights reflected at them from the water— alligator eyes lit by the light of the fire devouring the airboat and tree.

"How fast do alligators run?" he asked.

"Not as fast as they swim. But in a straight line, they can easily outrun a human in short bursts of speed."

"Okay. So we avoid the water, zigzag through the grass, pray we make it to the burning tree and hope that will keep them at bay until we figure something else out. That's my plan. I'm hoping you have a better one."

A beautiful smile lit up her whole face. "Ask and you shall receive. Listen. Do you hear that?"

He listened, and then he heard. The jet-engine whir of an airboat fan. Seconds later, powerful searchlights flickered over them.

"Silver? Is that you?" Buddy Johnson's gravelly voice called out.

She waved her hand in the air, grinning like a kid.

"I never thought I'd be happy to see another airboat," Colton said.

Less than a minute later they were on the boat, laughing and shaking hands with their rescuers—Buddy Johnson and three other men whom Colton had seen at Callahan's before but whose names he didn't remember, with Danny Thompson at the wheel.

As Danny turned the boat back toward Mystic Glades, Buddy handed bottles of water to Colton and Silver from a cooler. "That'll be four dollars. Each."

"Put it on my tab," Colton growled.

Buddy laughed and slapped his shoulder. "It's on me. I'm just glad we could help, that Charlie stopped in at Callahan's and—"

"Wait, he didn't go to the interstate to call the police like I told him?"

"Didn't have to. He said he kept checking for bars on the phone as he headed into Mystic Glades and voilà, bars. He made the call and swung over to Callahan's. So your boss is on his way. Oh, he said he'd meet you there, at the bar. But he put a call out to get some state troopers out here and some kind of rescue team or other. I imagine they're already out looking for those fellas from that camp. They won't get away."

"Once they're all rounded up," Colton said, "they'll start falling like dominoes all over each other to squeal on their boss in return for a lighter sentence. We'll have the head of the drug operation, and Eddie's killer, in no time. Hopefully some of the cocaine in that shed we torched survived the fire to be used as evidence." He shrugged. "But if not, I'm sure there's enough residue and eyewitnesses to overcome that."

"And the robbery ring will be stopped, too," Silver said.

Colton grimaced. "I suppose you'll want me to speak for the boys and try to get any charges against them dropped in return for their testimony against the drug dealers."

She patted his chest. "Of course."

He kissed her. "I suppose I could do that for you."

The airboat slowed, then bumped gently against the dock.

"We're home," Danny announced, and tied off the boat.

Silver hugged him and smiled. "Thank you. And thank you, Buddy. Thank you all. Colton and I weren't looking forward to a night with the gators."

They headed through the path to the street, talking about everything that had happened. When the group reached the street in front of the B and B, Silver tugged Colton to the side.

"I'm filthy. I'm going to get a shower. And I want to check on Tippy and Jenks. They're probably pulling their hair out by now. Neither of them ever expected to have to run everything completely on their own. You go on ahead to

Callahan's to meet up with Drew and I'll join you in a few minutes."

He hesitated, and looked toward the inn, which was all lit up, with the lights on throughout the bottom floor and some of the rooms on the second. He reminded himself that there were tons of people—eight bedrooms' worth—in the B and B. She wouldn't be alone. He had nothing to worry about.

Buddy turned toward him. "You coming, Colton? That boss of yours is probably already waitin' on you by now."

"Go," Silver said. "I'll be fine." She didn't wait for his response. She hurried down the walkway and up the steps, then waved before heading inside. She pulled back the curtains from one of the front windows, blowing him a kiss before ducking back inside.

Buddy patted Colton on the back, urging him toward Callahan's. "You can wash up at the bar. Why don't you go ahead and tell me how you and Silver met? The grapevine says you're friends from way back. But I don't remember her mentioning you before."

Not wanting to go into the details about being undercover, Colton steered the conversation to questions about Buddy's mini-empire in Mystic Glades. Once he got Buddy talking about how to make money, he didn't stop. Which suited Colton just fine.

He noted his Mustang was parked in front of Callahan's and, thankfully, didn't look the worse for wear—not that he could see in the dark anyway. Daylight might show another story altogether.

Once he stepped inside the bar, he was surprised by how full it was. Nearly every table was taken. And J.J. was running around with heavy trays of food and beer, laughing and flirting with all the customers. He noticed Charlie at a table in the far corner, laughing with some girls. He was probably bragging about his exploits and no doubt embellishing them considerably.

Freddie hurried up to him and looked as though she was going to hug him, which was a scary thought in itself, but she wrinkled her nose and stopped a few feet away. "There's a utility sink in the back of the kitchen. You might want to rinse off some of that mud in there. Here, I'll show you."

She tugged him through the swinging kitchen doorway, which he didn't mind, since Buddy was left with his friends, extolling his genius and how to take advantage of the current tourist market.

Two cooks were running around at full speed, slapping burgers on the grill and throwing nachos in a pizza oven. When they stopped near the back door, Freddie waved him to the big, square sink with a hose hooked up to the faucet, which he eagerly took advantage of. There was a drain in the floor back here, so he washed off while she leaned against the far wall by the back door.

"Heard you and Silver had a busy night. Where is she?"

"At the B and B, washing up." He grabbed the bar of soap sitting on the top of the sink and lathered up his hands. "You're having a busy night, too. I don't think I've ever seen the place so full."

"Yeah, well, Tippy and Jenks about reached their limit trying to feed and take care of all those people at the inn, so I told 'em to bring them on up here for dinner."

Colton hesitated with his hands under the running water. He nodded at one of the cooks who hurried through and headed out the back door. "You're saying all the guests are here?"

"That's what I'm sayin'."

He grabbed some paper towels and dried his hands. "What about Tippy and Jenks? Are they at the B and B?"

"Nah, they're in the bar. Is there a problem?"

He shrugged. Maybe, maybe not. He didn't like the idea of Silver being alone, not with the boss of the drug-running operation still at large. He hurriedly dried off as best he could.

A knock sounded on the back door. Freddie propped the door open for the cook to bring in a large box that he must have gotten from a storage area outside.

Colton stepped past the door to go through the kitchen, then froze. Sitting in the parking lot behind the bar was a sky blue Mercedes, an old-fashioned one, from the eighties. And he'd just bet it was a diesel. "Freddie, whose car is that?"

She leaned around the door. "Cato drives it mostly."

"Mostly? Who else drives it?"

"Danny, sometimes. As a matter of fact, I think he drove it tonight."

Danny, the airboat captain. One of the new people Buddy had hired for the summer, right around the time the robbery and drug rings started up. And he knew these canals and waterways. He also knew every new person who came or went, courtesy of his role as boat captain bringing tourists to and from Mystic Glades. Hanging out while waiting for the tourists to have their "free" meal before a tour, he'd hear any gossip from the townspeople. He'd know everything going on.

And he'd been in the boat tonight, hearing Colton and Silver talk about the operation being over, about men testifying against their boss. He'd also heard them talk about destroying the cache of drugs. Which meant he knew it was over, that he had nothing to lose.

And every reason to hate him and Silver.

"Where is he?" He hurried through the kitchen toward the bar.

"Who?" Freddie called out after him.

"Danny."

"In the bar as far as I know."

He shoved the swinging door open and it slammed back on its hinges, making J.J. jump in surprise as she approached the door.

"Whoa, slow down there, Mr. Graham. What's the hurry?"

"Danny," he said. "The boat captain. Where is he?" He scanned the bar, searching the groups of people around the room.

"I don't know. Look around. I'm sure he's here somewhere. Everyone else seems to be." She laughed and headed into the kitchen.

Buddy turned from a conversation with someone sitting on a bar stool. "You lookin' for Danny?"

"You know where he is?"

"Didn't you notice? He stayed with the boat. Said he had to refuel it and get it ready for the morning tour."

The swinging doors at the front banged against the wall as a man ran inside, gasping for breath. "Fire!" he choked. "The B and B's on fire!"

The crack of a gunshot boomed like thunder from outside.

Silver! Colton almost knocked the man over

as he ran through the doors and leaped off the boardwalk. He pumped his arms and legs, sprinting as fast as he could toward the inn and praying all the way.

Let her be okay. Please, please, God, let her be okay.

Chapter Sixteen

Colton slid to a halt, shielding his face from the heat of the flames. The entire bottom floor was already engulfed. And the heat was so intense he couldn't get closer than about twenty feet from the structure.

"Silver! Where are you? Silver!" He ran around the perimeter, looking up at the second floor, which was belching smoke. The windows had already exploded from the heat.

He was vaguely aware that men were running around him and that Buddy was barking orders about some kind of pump system and hoses, something about running them to the marsh for a water supply.

"Silver!" Colton yelled again, desperately looking for a way inside. He ran to the back, dodging men who were running hoses to the rear of the property. He cupped his hands around his mouth. "Silver!"

"Here! Colton! I'm here!"

Silver. He frantically spun around, trying to figure out where her voice was coming from.

"Up here!"

He shaded his eyes from the glow of the fire and looked up. Silver leaned out the attic window, and even from that distance he could see she was covered in blood.

"Hold on!" He ran along the back, desperately looking for any way to climb up to her. He grabbed Buddy as he and Charlie ran by with what looked to be a fire hose, although no water was coming out of it. "Buddy, a ladder. Do you have a ladder?"

"Why?"

He pointed at Silver.

"Dear God. No, nothing I have would reach that high. The whole bottom floor is engulfed. We couldn't use a ladder even if we had one tall enough."

A hair-raising roar had them whirling around.

Charlie pointed to the enormous oak tree in the middle of the yard. "Is that a panther up there?"

The same black panther that Colton had seen twice before sat on a thick limb, halfway up the tree. But it wasn't the panther that caught Colton's attention. It was the thick vines hanging down beside the large cat that had hope bursting inside his chest. He took off and leaped up for the bottom branch, hauling himself up into the tree.

"What are you doing?" Buddy called up. "That tree's too far from the house to do you any good."

Colton ignored him and scrambled up the tree, a good climbing tree as Silver had said, with thick, sturdy branches. The panther hissed at him when he got near it, but he paid it no mind, climbing higher and higher, until he was a good ten feet higher than the attic window. Below him, he saw Charlie climbing up, as well.

A burst of heat flared out from the house as the greedy flames began to consume the second floor. Black smoke started billowing out the attic window. Silver clung to the sill, leaning out with a towel over her face to filter out the smoke.

"I'll be right there!" he yelled. The vines that had been hanging below by the panther were too short to reach the house. He selected another vine and pulled his knife out of his boot, using it to hack the lower part of the vine free.

"No, that one's too thick. You won't have a good handhold." Charlie had just reached a branch below his. "This one. Use this one."

Colton immediately cut the vine loose that Charlie had pointed to and yanked on it. It seemed strong and well anchored. He looped his hand through one of the knots formed by the vine's intricate stem.

"Over there." Charlie pointed. "You need a good running start. Climb to that branch there, then run and jump."

Colton leaped to the other branch. It was thinner than the others and bowed beneath him. He cartwheeled his arms, to regain his balance.

"Colton! Be careful!" Silver yelled, her voice hoarse and raspy.

"Get ready!" He moved as far out on the branch as he dared, got a good hold on the vine, then took off running toward the other side of the tree.

"Now!" Charlie yelled. "Jump!"

He dove off the branch. The vine jerked and held and swung him toward the attic at a dizzying speed. He lifted his feet to clear the window and suddenly he was inside, falling onto the floor. But before he could stop it, the vine slipped from his grasp and jerked back toward the opening.

"Silver, the vine!" He lunged toward the window as she made a grab for the vine.

She lost her balance and started to fall. "Colton!"

He grabbed her legs just before she could plummet down below and hauled her back in.

"I've got it. I've got it!" She held up the vine and gifted him with the most amazing smile he'd ever seen.

"You're incredible," he said, giving her a quick kiss. He wanted to check her injuries, stanch the bleeding, but there was no time. The floor beneath them was bowing from the heat on the second floor and could collapse any second.

"We have to jump."

Her face turned pale and she coughed. "I know."

He picked her up in his arms. "Wrap your legs around my waist and your arms around my neck. And hold on. Don't let go."

She tucked her face against his neck. "I won't let go."

He looped his hands through the vine and climbed onto the sill.

An explosion sounded behind them and searing heat blasted out at them.

"Now!" He leaped out of the window.

The vine jerked, and then they were swinging toward the tree. Charlie reached out for them, grabbing the vine as they came close and helping Colton haul them both onto the branch.

"Oh, my God," Silver whispered. "Oh, my God. I can't believe we just did that."

Another explosion sounded behind them and they looked back. Flames shot through the attic window where they'd just been standing.

"Ever heard the expression in the nick of time?" Silver teased.

Colton laughed and hugged her close.

She coughed and he pulled back to look at her. "The blood—"

"Is mostly Danny's, but some of it's mine. I'll explain later. Can we get out of this tree, please?"

But some of it's mine. Those words sent a chill deep inside Colton. He clasped her close. "Charlie, we need another vine."

"Already planned on that." He held out a vine that hung all the way to the ground.

Colton grabbed it and wrapped his legs around the bottom to use as a brake. With Silver holding on, he shimmied them down to the ground. Charlie did the same and landed right beside them on another vine.

Colton scooped Silver up in his arms. "Charlie, we need a ride to the hospital."

"You got it, boss."

Charlie took off toward the front and Colton carried his precious cargo in his arms as he made his way through the gauntlet of makeshift firefighters pumping swamp water onto the B and B.

Silver coughed again, black soot staining her skin beneath her nose, and closed her eyes.

"Hold on, sweetheart," Colton said. "Hold on."

Chapter Seventeen

Silver hated hospitals, and this one in Naples was no different. Actually, it was worse. Because in addition to being poked, prodded and fussed over for the better part of two days, she'd been interviewed over and over and over again. Not just by the police, but also by DEA agents and the FBI, all hoping that they'd be able to close several open investigations that all centered on Danny Thompson. They wanted to know everything that he'd done. And how he'd died.

"I've told you this several times already," she said to the investigator sitting on the left side of her hospital bed.

A warm hand gently feathered down the right side of her face. Colton. He leaned over the bed and kissed her. "I promise this is the last question you have to answer today. Just tell Special Agent Williams what you already told me about Thompson."

She let out an impatient breath and relayed how she'd started upstairs for a shower when she smelled some kind of fuel, which turned out to be the boat fuel that Thompson had spread around the foundation of the inn. He'd started the fire, and she ran for the front door to get out. But he'd stopped her and they'd fought. He'd blocked her way out but hadn't anticipated how quickly the fire would consume everything. He ended up trapped just like her.

"We ran from the fire, up the stairs. I knew I had a gun in my room in the attic, so when I fought my way free of him, I ran up there. He followed me and I shot him."

"In self-defense?" Williams asked.

"Of course it was." Silver frowned at the other woman. "Are we done here?"

"Just a few more questions."

Silver groaned and thumped her head back on the pillow.

"Tomorrow," Colton said, ushering the agent out of the room. "Come back tomorrow to finish your interview."

Williams sputtered and protested, but Colton was determined, and soon it was just the two of them left in the room. Which Silver belatedly realized wasn't necessarily a good thing. Because from the way he'd been doting on her, since finishing all his interviews, she knew he wasn't going to like anything she had to say.

He sat in the seat Williams had vacated and took her hand. "You're breathing better."

"Yep. All the smoke is gone."

He gently smoothed her bangs back. "Your stitches look good. I bet you won't even have a scar from where that jerk hit you. If Thompson were still alive, I'd pay him back for that."

"Well, he's not. So that's one less thing you have to do for me." She tugged her hand free from his.

He frowned. "What's wrong? And don't say 'nothing.' I know you. Something's definitely bothering you."

She let out a long breath. "You don't know me, Colton. *That's* what's bothering me. You should be getting on with your life instead of camping out in my hospital room."

The smile faded from his face and he searched her eyes. "What's this about?"

"I'm just...we've only known each other for a few days. And all of it was under extraordinary circumstances. Neither of us really knows each other."

"Well, of course we do. Extraordinary circumstances means we experienced a lot in a short amount of time. I care about you, Silver. Very much. And I...why are you shaking your head? You think I don't care?"

She twisted her fingers in the blanket covering her, hating what she had to do. Nothing had ever seemed this hard, because she cared far too much for him, so much that her heart was breaking. But she knew this was the right thing.

She had to let him go.

"Silver—"

"I think you should leave."

He froze. "What?"

"You heard me. Colton, I owe you my life. I owe the future of my hometown to you. You saved us, the Jones family, those kids, and we all owe you a debt of gratitude. But you and I, well, there's no future for us. We need to call it like it is."

"Call it like it is? What's wrong? Are you upset that I haven't said that I love you? I thought it was obvious, but I'll say it. I—"

"No. Don't say it."

He frowned. "What's really going on here?"

She blinked back the moisture in her eyes. "Don't you see? You think you…care about me…because of everything that has happened.

But two people can't fall in love after only a few days. I don't know anything about you. And you know little about me. I've never met your family, know nothing about how you grew up, who your friends are, what you do for fun. None of it's real."

He waved his hand in the air. "All those things—our pasts, our families, how we grew up—they made us who we are today, who we are right now. And we do know each other. I know that you're creative, and smart, and care deeply about people, especially young people. I suspect you love babies and I bet you want a houseful someday."

"You suspect, but you don't know that."

"If you're worried that we're going too fast—"

"I am."

His frown smoothed out with relief. "If that's all you're worried about, no problem. When you get out of here we'll date. I'll take you to movies and restaurants, learn your favorite foods. And we can go visit our families."

"Colton. You work undercover, for months at a time. And you love it. I don't want to be the cause of you giving that up. You aren't ready to settle down, or even start a family."

"How would you know that?"

"Because when your boss, Drew, interviewed me, we talked about you, too. And he told me what a fine detective you are, and how much you love your job. That you planned to work undercover for at least several more years."

His eyebrows dipped down. "He had no business discussing my career decisions or my future plans with you. He doesn't know what I want."

"What do you want? To sit at a desk? You'd miss all the excitement of going undercover, of living a secret life, of trying to trick the bad guys and make that big score when you bring down an operation. I know. I've been there. I know the rush and how exciting it can be. But I'm done with all that. I'm ready to settle down, which is why I started the B and B." She grimaced. "Which I'll now have to rebuild. But my point is, you're not at that place. You aren't ready to settle down."

"You said we don't know each other. But you claim to know what I want, or don't want?"

She sighed. "You're right. I don't know. But I do know this. You never talked to your boss about getting out of undercover work until after you met me. I've been through this before. I've been that girl with a guy who changed his life, who gave up his dreams, so they could be together after a whirlwind romance. I married him, Colton."

He blanched. "You're married?"

"What? Oh, no, no, no. Of course not. Not anymore. We got married right out of high school. And within a few months, he was already resenting me, hating me, for everything he gave up to be with me. He'd lost a football scholarship in another state because he knew I didn't want to live there. And then he held that against me. It was horrible. That psychological abuse I mentioned? That's what I was talking about. We were divorced after six months. And I don't ever want to do that again. I do care about you, very much. But we have different dreams. And I don't want you giving yours up for me, and then hating me for it."

"I could never hate you," he said softly.

"You don't know that."

An awkward silence filled the room.

He stared across the bed, out the window. "You've given this a lot of thought, haven't you?"

"I have. Yes." And it was killing her inside to let him go. But she could never live with herself knowing she'd destroyed his dreams. Even if it destroyed hers by telling him goodbye.

He finally rose and leaned down and kissed her on the top of the head. His incredible blue eyes were unreadable as he looked down at her. His mouth worked, as if he was trying to come up with the perfect words to change her mind. But then he gave her a stiff nod and turned away.

And walked right out of her life.

"A TAD TO the left, Charlie," Silver called out as Charlie and Ned stood on ladders beside the front steps, holding either end of the blue, bed-shaped sign that announced, Under the Covers Bed & Breakfast, proprietor Silver Westbrook.

"Looks perfect where it is, if you ask me."

She smiled at Tippy standing beside her. "You think so?"

"I do."

"That's it," she called out. "Perfect."

Charlie gave her a thumbs-up, and soon the sound of hammers once again echoed through Mystic Glades. It had taken four long months to rebuild, but finally the inn was ready again.

"They're here." Tippy pointed up the road.

Silver turned to see a string of cars heading down Main Street. She checked her watch.

"They're early. The Larson family must be in an awful hurry to start their reunion."

"I think it's so exciting that one family booked the whole inn for two weeks. This is going to be fun."

Silver gave her a hug. "And since you have your degree now, you're totally prepared if I ditch you again and you're stuck taking care of everyone, right?" At the look of panic on Tippy's face, Silver laughed. "Don't worry. J.J. will be here soon. I promised I'd get you some real help this time, and I have. And I don't plan on going anywhere."

A flash of pain shot through her as a memory of Colton floated through her mind, but she held on to her smile to face her arriving guests. "Tippy, hurry inside. You'll need to register everyone."

"Yes, ma'am." She grinned and hurried down the walkway.

"Miss Westbrook?" A beautiful young woman

with striking blue eyes stopped in front of her and held out her hands.

"Please, call me Silver. You must be Celia?"

A smile lit the woman's eyes, painfully reminding Silver of another pair of blue eyes.

"That's right, Celia Larson." She suddenly wrapped Silver in a tight hug. "I'm so glad to meet you."

Silver stiffened, then laughed and hugged the woman back. "Nice to meet you, too. Please go on inside. Tippy will help you find your room."

Celia pulled back, squeezed her hand, then hurried off with the others, who were lugging their suitcases into the inn. When everyone was inside, and Charlie and Ned had folded up their ladders and headed up the street to return them to Buddy's store, Silver remained in front of the inn. She wanted a few more minutes to compose herself before facing the lovely, happy family inside.

To a person, every single one of them had smiled and waved at her as they went into the inn. She'd adored them all on the spot and looked forward to getting to know them. But first, she had to tamp down the melancholy that always overcame her whenever something reminded her of Colton, as young Celia's eyes had done. He was never far from her thoughts. And the feelings she'd had for him, that she hadn't trusted because they'd come too hard, too fast? They'd only grown stronger in his absence. She now knew that she was hopelessly in love with him. And although she'd go on with her life and find joy in other things—like getting to know the Larson family—she knew she'd always have a hollow place in her heart for the only man she'd ever really loved.

The throaty sound of an engine roared from up the street. She turned, and her heart gave a little lurch when she saw a black Mustang GT coming down the road toward her.

It couldn't be. Could it?

The car pulled into the only free spot, two

spaces away. The engine cut off. The door opened. And out stepped Colton Graham.

Silver pressed her hand against her thundering heart and took a step toward him, before she caught herself. Just because she now knew she'd made a mistake in letting him go didn't mean it was a mistake for him. She'd given him his dream back or, rather, she hadn't taken it away. He was doing what he wanted with his life. And she shouldn't read anything into the fact that he was here. They'd been friends once, briefly. So maybe that was what he was doing, just checking up on an old friend.

She just hoped she could survive seeing him again without breaking down into a puddle at his feet.

He got out of the car and literally took her breath away. His wavy, shoulder-length hair had been cut short, but not too short. And although she'd loved his wild hair, the new cut fit his personality better and emphasized the gorgeous angles of his face. Yes, she liked him like this. Loved him.

He took off his dark sunglasses and tossed them through the open window of the car, never taking his eyes off her. The cooler weather now had him wearing a leather jacket over his black T-shirt and black jeans. And his boots, shined to a high gloss, echoed on the pavement as he strode toward her, stopping so close she could feel the heat of him and had to crane her neck back to meet his gaze.

"Hello, Silver." His deep voice stroked goose bumps across her skin.

"Colton. You look…good."

He grinned. "You look amazing."

She couldn't help smiling. "And you're just as charming as ever."

He gestured toward the sign. "You changed the name. And the color."

"I wanted a fresh start."

His smile faded and he turned to face her. "Me, too." He held out his hand. "I don't think we've been correctly introduced. Colton Graham was my undercover name. My real name is Cole."

She shook his hand, feeling a bit stunned. "Cole. And your last name?"

He hesitated, and in that moment she suddenly knew.

"Larson," he said. "My name is Cole Larson."

She blinked. "Your…your family…they're…"

"Inside your inn right now. Yep. Pretty much every last one of them. Well, there are some aunts and uncles back in Jacksonville who didn't make the trip down, but my three brothers, sister, mom and dad, plus a few nieces and nephews made it. I imagine you remember Celia. She wouldn't have passed up the opportunity to meet you. And I'm told we look a lot alike."

She blinked again, still reeling. "Celia. Her eyes, that dark hair. Twins?"

He nodded.

"Then she's—"

"The artist. Yes. I didn't lie about that."

"I see." She shook her head. "No, no, I don't see. Colton… Cole…what are you doing here? And why is your family here?"

His hands shook as he reached for her, but then he stopped and dropped them to his side. "I tried to stay away, to forget you, since it was what *you* wanted. But it was never what *I* wanted. I went back undercover and hated it. I quit my job."

She drew in a sharp breath. "You quit? You're not a police officer anymore?"

"Oh, I'm still a detective. I'm just not doing undercover work anymore. Which means I have fairly regular hours, except for the occasional callout. And I've discovered that I like that. No, actually, I love it. I was ready to make that change, Silver. I was wearing myself down undercover all the time. Now I'm discovering the life that was passing me by." He waved toward the inn. "And rediscovering my family. I've spent a lot of time with them over the past few months."

He raised a hand, and this time he didn't stop. He cupped the side of her face, his fingers shaking as they feathered across her skin. "I've talked of little else but you to them, and they got pretty sick and tired of it. They told me I was a fool if I didn't go after you, beg you if I had to, to give us a chance. Because you haven't taken my dreams away, Silver. You've given me a new dream, of a future with a wonderful, beautiful woman who takes such pleasure from the simplest things, and makes me see the world through her artist's eyes."

He cupped her face with his hands. "I. Love. You. It wasn't a fluke, or an infatuation because we shared some intense experiences. It's stronger, brighter, than it was the day I left the hospital. All I'm asking is that you give us a chance. Date me. Get to know me, my past." He waved toward the inn again. "My family. And if you still don't feel the way that I feel, it will probably kill me, but I'll go. I'll walk away if that's what you want. Because your happiness is what matters most to me. I love you. You're everything to me."

A sob burst from her lips and she wrapped her arms around his waist. "Colton... Cole... oh, good grief, I'll never get that right."

He laughed and tightened his arms around her. "Call me anything you want if it makes you happy."

She pulled back and slid her hands up around his neck. "You...you make me happy. I was an idiot for making you go away. I've been miserable ever since."

His eyes bored into hers with an intensity that took her breath away. "What are you saying?"

Tears tracked down her face now, unchecked. She smiled and threaded her fingers through the gently curling wisps of hair at the nape of his neck. "I'm saying that I love you, Colton Cole Graham Larson. I have from the moment I looked into those incredible blue eyes of yours. And I'd love nothing more than to meet your family, learn about your past. But it doesn't really matter." She flattened her palm over his chest. "What matters is what's in here, the person you are today, and that you love me, too."

The smile that lit his face, his eyes, was like sunlight rising over a beautiful field of flowers, painting happiness and joy across the land and across Silver's heart.

"I love you, Silver." His voice was thick with emotion. "I love you."

"Shut up and kiss me."

He laughed, and then he was kissing her and making her toes curl inside her shoes, melting her from the inside out. All too soon he pulled back. She sighed with disappointment.

He glanced at the inn, his face falling. "Damn."

"What?" She followed his gaze, but she didn't see anything alarming. "Is something wrong?"

"My family. My *mom* and *dad* are here. And all I want to do is make love to you."

She beamed up at him and grabbed his hand in hers, tugging him toward the B and B. "There'll be time for that later. Promise. Come on. Introduce me to your family."

He grinned and scooped her up in his arms. She laughed the whole way to the door. And then he carried her across the threshold.

* * * * *

MILLS & BOON®

Why shop at millsandboon.co.uk?

Each year, thousands of romance readers find their perfect read at millsandboon.co.uk. That's because we're passionate about bringing you the very best romantic fiction. Here are some of the advantages of shopping at www.millsandboon.co.uk:

* **Get new books first**—you'll be able to buy your favourite books one month before they hit the shops

* **Get exclusive discounts**—you'll also be able to buy our specially created monthly collections, with up to 50% off the RRP

* **Find your favourite authors**—latest news, interviews and new releases for all your favourite authors and series on our website, plus ideas for what to try next

* **Join in**—once you've bought your favourite books, don't forget to register with us to rate, review and join in the discussions

Visit **www.millsandboon.co.uk**
for all this and more today!